Casino Queen

by

Cara Bertoia

Casino Queen

Cover Art by *Diana Carlile*

The Wild Rose Press, Inc.
PO Box 708
Adams Basin, NY 14410-0708
Visit us at www.thewildrosepress.com

Publishing History
First Edition, 2022
Trade Paperback ISBN 978-1-5092-4091-3
Digital ISBN 978-1-5092-4092-0

Published in the United States of America

A few days after a surprise rainstorm, the landscape erupted in wildflowers. Indian paintbrush, ocotillo, and purple mat along with a score of other blooms painted the desert floor in all shades of the rainbow. Caroline gazed out the window, admiring the countryside as she drove down the hill past the gun range, around the corner, and onto the road leading to the casino. Her car meandered down the nearly empty highway of the High Desert, on her way to work, slowly enough to enjoy the glorious day. Stopping at the locally owned donut shop, she took her time choosing a wide variety of tasty treats for the staff. Small gestures like bringing donuts were always a big hit in the employee lounge.

Back on the road, her eyes followed the arc of a bald eagle flying across the brilliant blue sky. The eagle landed on the far-left corner of the Night Hawk billboard, which stood above the road, fourteen feet high and forty-eight feet wide, enticing travelers to eat, play, win!

Glancing upward she did a double take. A new message painted across the front read, '*Caroline Popov must die!*' in red paint, ten feet high. In disbelief she slammed on her brakes, pulled over to the curb shifting the car in park. She wanted to make sure she had read it right.

PRAISE FOR CARA BERTOIA AND . . .

Cruise Quarters:

"…A novel About Casinos and Cruise Ships was chosen Tripatini.com 'Read of the Week'.

~*~

"…An amazing travel novel which is as much about romance as it is about travel…"

The Review Girl blog

~*~

Named one of the seventeen best books for travelers at Get in the Hot Spot Blog.

~*~

Camino De Santiago—The Walker's Guide:

"…Their fantastic video captures the Camino, the sound of the wind and the rain and banter of meeting new friends. Far superior to any guidebook . . ."

Ultreya Website

~*~

Dedication

To my wonderful husband Ray who has always
encouraged my creative endeavors

Chapter One

Twentynine Palms, California, March 2019

Caroline Popov's eyes turned upward, taking one last look at the California sky laced with the red streaks of sunrise. Glancing at the large neon sign hoisted on the roof, flashing *Night Hawk* in bold blue letters, she stopped to inhale one last breath of clean air before stepping on a rubber pad.

Immediately, large heavy doors slid open, revealing an ugly but functional square, squat interior, with no windows or clocks on the walls. She entered perpetual night. The carpet, a colorful jumble of geometric shapes guaranteed to hide dirt, covered a concrete floor. An elegant chandelier hung from the ceiling. She studied the space, the table games pit, consisting of blackjack and carnival games, dominated the middle of the room, surrounded by thousands of slot machines.

The universal noise of casinos greeted her, slot machines pinged and dinged while customers blindly pulled the handles. As lucky sevens, cherries, and shamrocks lined up in rows, bells and whistles rang out, announcing winners, small rewards all designed to keep the 'guest' engaged.

Caroline tried to name that tune, a classic pop hit from the nineties playing in the background. The sounds were muted, the volume of the slot machines would be cranked up later in the day. Most casino floors were relatively empty in the wee small hours of the morning. She found it hard to distinguish the early birds from the players who had spent the night chasing a dream. She bent down to pick up dirty glasses which had been deposited haphazardly at empty slot machines. The untidiness would have to be addressed, but not now. Young men sporting buzz cuts, good posture, and fresh faces, all signs of new Marines, seated at the long bar positioned across the back wall waited patiently for first call. She checked her watch, three minutes until the bar opened at six a.m.

Cautious, she stopped a fair distance away to observe the action in the pit where nine table games arranged in a semi-circle were anchored by a roulette game at the end. At the nearest blackjack table, a young guy, hair pulled back in a man bun and wearing a tight T-shirt, slapped his hand on the table yelling, "*Merde!*"

He must have lost, she thought, as she tested how much of her high school French she retained.

A young woman, obviously a winner, jumped up and screamed, "*J'ai gagné!*"

The slim, pretty couple both dressed in Euro grunge. She envied the way the French exuded style even on a camping trip and surmised they were camping at Joshua Tree, the national park twenty miles down the road. The Night Hawk situated on the road halfway between the world's largest Marine base and the national park in an area known as the High Desert.

Caroline had worked long and hard to secure her new position as casino general manager. She needed to stand still and take a deep breath, shrugging off the fact that a casino might be one of the last places in America where an employer was legally allowed to expose its employees to toxic levels of cigarette smoke. Comfortable with the familiar setting of her life, the haze of cigarette smoke, the smell of stale beer, and the canned music wafting through the air, most of the time she didn't notice any of it, but today she savored it. Casino life didn't suit everyone, but in a strange way it did fit her.

Lost in thought, she found herself caught by surprise when a strong hand suddenly reached around her waist, giving it a squeeze. "Look who I found. An early bird making a great impression on her first day."

She'd recognize that voice anywhere, the slow soft cadence common to the Native American tribes of the Southwest. Turning, she encountered a rugged face, a countenance saved from bland handsomeness by a scar across the chin.

She stood at just under six feet, John Tovar a few inches over. With her good pair of work heels on, three inches to be exact, they stood eye to eye. As always, those sleepy blue eyes against his oak-colored skin were mesmerizing, those eyes had seduced a thousand women. Aware of his own appeal, he used it well and often. The long jet-black braid falling down his back only added to the mystique of John Tovar. His looks, coupled with the knowledge that he was the chairman of one of the wealthiest tribes in America, caused women to fall hard.

"Hello, boss," she said, and immediately broke eye contact.

Even after all these years, the charisma in his eyes made her nervous, worried if she gazed at him too long it would be like staring at the sun. She would be blinded. Over the years she'd trained herself to be immune from his charms. She had decided long ago her mentor could not be her lover. She had tried that once. Where had it gotten her? Well, here, actually. But she would not make the same mistake again.

"I thought I would come and lend you some moral support." He spoke as if he chose every word deliberately. But as he spoke, she caught a whiff of gin on his breath.

She smiled as she answered, "Hey, the fact that this is the only bar in town, and it just opened…only a happy coincidence."

"You got me. But since I'm here, use me as you will. Let me introduce you to the team. Watch out for knives. Everyone who applied for your job will try to stab you in the back."

They chatted as they walked the gaming floor. "The Shotowa Tribe has big plans for this place." John glanced around the casino. "The Palm Oasis has always been our top priority. But now the tribe is turning its attention to the Night Hawk. Our plan is to modernize, bring this casino into this century."

When John had told her of his plan to promote her, no one was as anxious as she to prove what she could accomplish. She realized what a privilege she had been given, to have free rein to reorganize a casino, always aware her promotion made her one of the few female casino managers in the country. She wanted to score a big hit in honor of all the qualified women who had never gotten their chance.

"I can't wait until we install the new computer system for the table games."

"Sure," he agreed. "But why did I transfer you up from Palm Springs to be my Casino Queen?"

"Casino Queen, really? Apparently, you are the only person in America who isn't watching the show about the seven kingdoms on cable. The queens always get killed in the most horrific ways. They are hanged, beheaded, poisoned, burned alive in an explosion, or have their throat slit."

"I promise that won't happen to you." He gestured for her to take a seat at an empty 'Mystic Mermaid' slot machine, then sat across from her. They swiveled their chairs to face each other. John tried to act serious, but a smile kept pulling at the corner of his eyes. "According to the Mazurie decision, Native American tribes are considered sovereign nations. Therefore as leader of the tribe, I am King of the Shotowa."

He continued. "Believe me, when I met the Queen of England I was introduced as the leader of the Shotowa nation. Let me be clear, as soon as you drove into this parking lot you entered the nation." He gestured toward the uniformed officers standing at the door. "We have our own army."

She decided to play along with the flow of his logic. "You mean security guards."

"Precisely, trained courtesy of the United States Marine Corps. The tribe issues its own currency, gaming chips made of ceramic clay, stamped with our logo. At the cashiers' cage, our central bank, those chips can be exchanged for U.S. dollars. Anyone can find food in our three restaurants or the team member dining room for employees. An underground well supplies us with water. We provide hotel rooms for shelter. Any guest who comes to stay with us will find their basic human needs covered by the Shotowa Tribe. Never forget we are a sovereign nation. I am the king, and I anoint you Queen of the Night Hawk. But why did I choose you, out of all the maidens in the land to be our queen?"

"Because the last manager got fired for sexual harassment and you were pretty sure I wouldn't bang the bartender?" She smiled. "Let's get real, I am here because sometimes in casinos when management gets lax, the employees take advantage. It's my job to make sure everything is legit, and only someone from the outside can do that. You have to shake things up when the people on the inside get too comfortable. Did I get it right?"

He nodded his approval. "Never forget the Shotowa nation is depending on you. Do you solemnly swear to do all in your power to protect our assets?"

Feeling a bit ridiculous, she placed her hand over her heart and pledged allegiance to the Shotowa nation. "I do."

"Wonderful, I declare you an honorary Shotowa."

After she had been sworn in, they strolled to the table games pit where they were greeted by the table games manager. "John, what a surprise, a morning visit! Ms. Popov, so glad to finally meet you."

A slim man, Derrick Thomas, with a bulbous nose that looked like it had imbibed a thousand drinks too many offered a wicked smile. By now word would have gotten around. He knew who exactly who Caroline was. They all would.

He extended a slender hand attached to long bony fingers for her to shake. "Hello, I'm Derrick from Donegal. Top of the morning to you."

He piled on a brogue as thick as butter, but she could tell by the glint in his eyes he spoke pure blarney. He probably wondered why John had promoted her and might even believe they were having an affair. In Derrick's mind he should have been promoted to general manager. John had already told her that as table games manager Derrick from Donegal's name had been on the short list. Most importantly, he'd paid his dues.

It surprised her how many people, including herself, fought for a job where the average casino manager only survived around two years, the usual length of their contract, before being fired. She suspected Derrick wouldn't mind buttering her up until she too became toast.

"Please call me Caroline." They shook hands. Her expression tried to convey support while at the same time letting him know she was the boss.

"Now you're here. We are facing a bit of a kerfuffle this morning." Derrick tilted his head toward a thin, middle-aged Asian woman. The gesture hadn't been very subtle, but the customer was beyond noticing anything. "Jenny Chin keeps taking a kip at the table. She has been playing for twenty-four hours straight. She is one of our biggest players, but this is the second request for a five thousand dollar advance this week. She is already over her limit, so I need your approval to issue her the marker."

It hurt Caroline to watch Jenny Chin struggling, slumped over the table, her head resting on her left hand. Her hair hung in uncombed clumps around her face, coffee stains dotted the front of her oxford shirt. Her eyelids slowly closed as she studied the cards.

The dealer said, "Jenny, wake up. You know you

can't sleep at the table."

"I'm not asleep," Jenny mumbled as her eyelids slid closed.

Caroline asked, "Isn't she the player who just lost her husband in Afghanistan?"

"Yes, last month at the hotel bombing in Kabul."

Caroline had studied the profiles of the red card players—the high rollers—at the Night Hawk, well aware that the future of Jenny's play depended on stopping her before she got in too deep. It was hard to walk away from a winning streak, even harder to leave a losing one. Jenny exhibited all the telltale signs of an addict, long sessions at the table, asking for a larger credit line, an overall disheveled appearance. She suspected if she searched through her purse, she would find a fresh change of underwear stored there, one of the signs of a compulsive gambler, in it for the long haul. She made no attempt to keep it together, she had surrendered long ago. It was hard to deal with a player suffering the last stage of her gambling addiction, the one where she just wanted to lose all her money.

She knelt down beside her. "Jenny, I'm Caroline Popov, the new casino manager. After the hand, take a break. I'd like to buy you some breakfast so we can get to know each other better."

While Jenny slowly rose to her feet Caroline placed her hand on the crook of her elbow slowly leading her from the table. As they walked away from the pit she glanced back, John winked, a signal he approved of the way she handled the first problem of the day.

During breakfast she tried to decipher if Jenny seemed relieved or resigned to having left the blackjack table. Sometimes it was hard to tell. "Let's comp you a room at the hotel."

She extended the offer because she empathized with the frail woman. Caroline could remember the feeling of not wanting to go home and face the loneliness, but she was pleased because Jenny had managed to swallow a few bites of eggs and some toast.

She wanted to make sure every time a customer walked into the Night Hawk, they would find a warm welcoming place. Carefully she made her rounds of the gaming floor, stopping at slot machines to pick up ashtrays overflowing with cigarette butts, emptying them into the trash. It was always a good idea to pitch in to set a good example for the crew. She wanted them to see that she didn't mind getting her hands dirty. Next, she picked up empty glasses and carried them to the bar. As she deposited the dirty glasses at the workstation, her eyes were drawn to a voluptuous blonde with a classically beautiful face wedged between two Marines.

A security guard stood in front of the girl. "Crystal," he spoke in a frustrated tone, "I've told you before, you can't be scamming the customers for drinks or money. You know you're eighty-sixed from here. I gave you thirty days. Scoot before I make it sixty."

She wondered what angle the girl was working. In every casino people known as casino fleas operated their personal side businesses on the gaming floor. They settled in, made money without ever gambling or applying for a job. Crystal's body was covered in tattoos from the face down. A flower vine crawled up her neck, as if the vines were holding up her beautiful face. While the guard scolded her Crystal stood, revealing glitter hot pants. She pranced along the floor in red stilettos, quickly vanishing like a puff of smoke.

The security guard turned his attention to the young men, now that the object of their affection was gone. "Listen to me, guys," he spoke in a serious tone to the two young, naïve Marines. "She's in here every day. I can promise you the only thing either of you are going to get from her is the check."

After he finished his lecture, Caroline waved the security guard over. He approached her tentatively as if he was the one in trouble. When he stood in front of her she read his name engraved on the badge pinned to his chest. His uniform, designed to resemble a local police officer, looked smart, his shirt hugged his ripped chest. She could appreciate a little eye candy. "Great job, Jamar. The last thing we need are locals hustling the customers, even ones as gorgeous as she is. Not the best thing for business."

"Good morning, ma'am. Crystal is a dancer at the Goldbar, but it seems like she spends more time here than there. She may be gone for now but there are always lonely Marines, far from home for the first time, easy targets for a smart girl like her. She'll be back." Jamar blushed as he spoke. His buzz cut identified him as the burly ex-Marine he once was.

"Makes sense. I wondered what she did for a living with a body covered in tats." Suddenly she smiled, enjoying playing the lady boss. She couldn't recall the last time she had made a man blush.

She made her way upstairs to the security office to meet Brandon Boyd the security manager. "Hi, I'm Caroline Popov, the new casino manager. Introduce me to the people who have been eighty-sixed from this place. I want to be able to recognize them by sight."

His skin was the color of fine cocoa, his bald crown shined like a ceramic bowl, the remaining hair secured in a ponytail. Another rugged ex-Marine and ex-cop, a double threat. John had told her Brandon worked at the casino as a favor to him. He liked to keep the people he trusted close to him, and Brandon was his best friend. He trained every day to be fighting ready, which was a plus in a casino, when you never knew who might walk through the front doors itching for a fight.

He led her to a wall covered with photographs of a select group of ex-customers. "Up here we have a collection of hustlers, petty thieves, hookers, drug pushers, and gambling addicts, the finest the High Desert has to offer. You will get to know them intimately because they keep trying to sneak back in."

Together they began to study all the people who had been barred from the casino. Brandon commented, "Did you know eighty-sixed is a term left over from the Depression? A famous speakeasy was located on eighty-six Bedford Street in New York City. Many of its patrons were known to extricate themselves from the premises whenever the heat showed up. Only now the casino extricates the patrons."

"I always wondered where the term came from." It took a minute, but she located a picture of Crystal standing beside the bar and a caption, *Thirty day suspension, offense hustling.* "I ran into her this morning." She would have to memorize these faces. "I am always surprised how many young people decorate the wall of shame."

"What you consider the wall of shame, some

consider the wall of fame. Many men, and I'm sorry to say more and more women, consider getting eighty-sixed a rite of passage. Then they can brag about what bad asses they are, getting kicked out of a casino by security," Brandon added. "Keeps us busy up here."

****

After Caroline introduced herself to all the department heads, she made her way upstairs to her office. Working at her desk, plowing through the hundreds of e-mails on the company computer, her cell phone began to vibrate. Surveillance needed her downstairs to check out a problem at the cashier's cage.

Standing at the entrance to the cage door marked *Employees Only*, she gazed in awe as Joanna, the head of surveillance, lifted a broken cash sorter, a heavy machine, while Deanna, the head of cash operations, easily inserted its replacement. The substantial women looked incredibly similar—both dressed in identical polyester Night Hawk jackets, the uniform of management. As ugly as those jackets were, they were nothing compared to what the employees might turn up in if left to their own devices. John had warned her these were women she didn't want to piss off because they could track a rabbit, rope a cow, and wrestle better than all the guys on the reservation. Watching them work she agreed. She would be sure to handle them with kid gloves.

They were known throughout the casino as the Tovar twins though they weren't twins, but cousins to John Tovar. Both women wore their hair in heavy braids that hung over the counter as they worked. After watching them, she began to notice subtle differences between them. A gray streak framed Deanna's face.

Joanna's cheeks were covered in fine lines as if etched by the sand from the desert. Deanna's light and breezy demeanor contrasted with Joanna's more severe personality. They both spoke with the Shotowa accent. The twins exemplified the main objective of the tribe, to empower tribal members and to promote them to management. John not only wanted his tribe to own casinos, he also wanted tribal members to work there.

Deanna reached into a cash drawer and pulled out a hundred-dollar bill. Laying it on a counter, she swabbed it with a special money detector pen. "I noticed something funny about this bill. It didn't look right. As you can see the marks across the back are black."

Caroline picked up the bill to examine it. "It's counterfeit, all right. I'll make sure all the other casinos in the valley are notified. Are there any others?"

"We're swabbing the hundred-dollar bills, right now. After that we will rewind the surveillance tapes, to see if we can figure out who passed these phony bills." A series of surveillance cameras positioned around the casino recorded the action on every table game and slot machine in the joint. With a sigh, Deanna added, "Even though it is a felony to pass counterfeit bills, that never stops some fool from trying."

They all nodded their heads in agreement.

Mid-afternoon, a three-card poker player accused the casino of cheating because machines shuffled the cards at the carnival games, instead of the dealers. Carnival games was a term the casino used for niche games like three-card poker, Texas hold'em, or blackjack swap, fast paced games with bonus side bets that could pay off big. Like many players, he was convinced shuffle machines could manipulate the cards to guarantee the casino always won.

She tried to soothe the disgruntled customer. "If the players never won it would be bad for business. No one would ever return to the Night Hawk, would they? Would you really be gambling here now if you thought we cheated?"

Shuffle machines were completely legitimate, and the casino used them to speed up the action at the table, but a losing player just wanted something or someone to blame for his bad luck. The customer wasn't always right, but maybe he could be pacified.

On any given day, the lists of incidents in a casino were long. Being busy made time fly by, but at some point a manager had to stop because the problems kept coming, and the phone never stopped ringing. At nine p.m. she handed casino operations over to the manager on duty. Walking out the door, she guesstimated she had crisscrossed the casino floor a hundred times. Her feet dragged like lead weights attached to her legs. Her right hand ached from being shook by dozens of people who wanted to introduce themselves. Exhausted, dreading the drive down the twisty mountain highway to Palm Springs, she told herself she'd have to get a place close by the Night Hawk and vowed to stop by a real estate agency at lunch tomorrow.

The thing about working in a casino was the way it sucked out all your energy, and you never had time to think. The appeal of working in a casino was the way it sucked out all your energy, and you never had time to think about your life.

She was careful to try not to think about the past, hoping the future would take care of itself.

****

"Few Americans have visited Joshua Tree, making it one of the least known national parks even though it is the title of an album by U2." Sandra Schwartz turned her head toward Caroline. "Fortunately for us, Europeans have discovered it, and they love it here in the High Desert. They come for rock formations, native petroglyphs, and wide-open spaces but also to experience the extreme heat. Nothing excites a Brit more than one hundred and ten degrees in the shade."

Sandra a local real estate agent in her forties was working hard to sell the area, but as they climbed the foothills in her massive sport utility vehicle the vista sold itself. The scenery could provide the perfect backdrop for a car commercial, a brilliant blue sky framed with miles and miles of rust-colored hills, teeming with jagged rocks stacked on top of each other, resembling a giant game of Jenga. Caroline imagined if one rock was disturbed, the rest would all come tumbling down.

Sandra continued her narrative. "They named the park and trees after Joshua, from the Bible because the way the trees bend, resembling a person praying. I don't see it myself, but it's a great tourist draw. You will find all kind of characters live up here. The area is a haven for struggling artists from La La Land, snowbirds, and retired Marines. I was a painter in Los Angeles and moved up here because of this extraordinary scenery and the low cost of living. But I have to pay my bills, so now I show houses."

That explained the variety of houses they had passed climbing up the hill, some quite traditional, others designed in the shape of geodesic domes. They had passed a home decorated with large, welded art pieces, while next door abandoned pickup trucks littered the yard.

The SUV stopped in front of a small cabin which could have been built from stones torn from the nearby hills. Let this place be charming, she prayed as she climbed up the driveway to a verandah running the length of the front. She envisioned herself rocking on the porch gazing for hours at the stunning scenery. Inhaling a deep breath, she savored the sweet smell of the desert. Quiet filled the air, the only sound a soft breeze rustling the bushes.

French doors opened into a flagstone living room floor. "These appliances could be updated," Sandra commented as they surveyed the kitchen. She opened the door to the refrigerator. "No ice maker or microwave, but there is a double oven built into the wall which is a plus." The canary yellow appliances dated the room to the early eighties.

"With two ovens I could entertain someone, but I don't have a clue who that would be," Caroline said. "It's not the kitchen of my dreams, but I hardly ever cook so I think I can make do here."

The furniture in the cabin resembled an extended stay motel, neutral but non-offensive. She could live with that. The price sealed the deal, half the price for double the space of her studio in Palm Springs. Finally debt free, she envisioned adding personal touches to brighten up the place.

"I'll take it," she declared as she gazed across the valley.

"You have just leased your own little piece of the back of beyond," Sandra said. "Thirty miles and a world away from the nearest freeway."

On the way back down the hill Caroline told herself this was either a place to hide or find herself.

She just wasn't sure which she was trying to do.

Chapter Two

A Dealer Must Be Able to Perform Calculations Quickly and Accurately

With a few weeks as casino general manager under her belt, Caroline began to feel comfortable in her new position, her new casino, and her new home, but she missed the camaraderie of her first job at the Palm Oasis. The casino staff had taken her in when she had been lost. Shortly after learning to deal, she became fluent in the lingo and customs of the casino, and the job became her world. Most days after work in Palm Springs, the dealers headed to Slaherty's, a fake Irish pub down the road, to knock back Guinness, taking turns complaining about what an incompetent jerk the casino manager they worked for was. It was their major form of entertainment. She learned nothing bonded team members more than bitching about the boss.

She had climbed many steps up the management ladder before becoming a general manager, dealer, pit boss, shift boss, and table games director. Every step along the way, her paycheck got bigger and her circle of friends smaller. After her promotion to pit boss, some of her friends began to distance themselves from her. Conversations stopped when she entered the room. By the time she became the shift manager she wasn't invited for after work drinks at the bar. Now after her promotion, she was well aware that she had become the jerk, and the best way to handle the situation was to give her employees plenty of space to vent about her. There would be many changes in the future, and she expected a lot of venting.

She recalled a saying she once heard, *'Everyone wants better but no one wants change.'* If she wanted to succeed, it was imperative to keep herself somewhat aloof, and very professional. Her job description included studying the casino, implementing efficiencies, and getting rid of dead weight. Firing them became so much harder if you regularly had drinks with the dead weight at the bar down the road. Every day she studied one department at a time, watching, just watching, for what she wasn't sure, but she would know it when she found it.

Upstairs she waved as she passed by the back of the house employees working at their cubicles, attending to human resources, payroll, benefits, and all the other departments that kept the place running. Ducking into the bathroom she took one final check of herself in the bathroom mirror, at the new navy suit, her hair waving in all the right places. All in all, not too shabby.

Today reminded her of her first basketball game in high school. Not used to being the center of attention, she panicked when the ball was passed to her. She preferred to hang back and let her teammates take the lead. At halftime, her coach pulled her aside and told her to forget about being the middle school girl embarrassed about towering over the other girls. Coach advised her to use her height to her advantage. With that in mind, she straightened her shoulders and held her head high.

Entering the hall to the conference room she repeated Miss Pratt's mantra: *"Fake it till you make it because everyone else is."*

Conversation stopped and all eyes turned to Caroline as she claimed her seat at the table, but they were soon distracted by a booming voice.

"Sorry I'm late." A striking redhead whose curvaceous figure flattered a very tight dress, Lenore, the head of gaming, ran in, apologizing. Gaming was the department that watched the watchers. Investigations went through gaming. They were responsible for conducting employee background checks, issuing gaming licenses, and approving all procedure changes. Filled with tribal members, gaming worked closely with management. Every movement made in the casino was the direct result of a procedure written in a manual. Everything and everyone had to pass the approval of the gaming department.

Aware there was a fine line between arrogance and confidence, and she better find it fast. She felt comfortable with the managers one on one, but today she had called a meeting of all the supervisors responsible for the gaming activities on the casino floor. The majority of them were day one employees, some tribal, all of them older than her, everyone waiting for her state of the casino speech.

She took mental attendance—the Tovar twins, Joanna and Deanna, Brandon Boyd, the head of security, Paula Guy, the count room manager, a local who had lived all her life in the High Desert, Jesus Gonzales, the Mexican slot manager whose family migrated to the Coachella Valley to pick grapes but gravitated to the casino business because of the opportunities, and Derrick from Donegal, representing table games. These were her people. When she was not present at the casino, most of them could take over as manager on duty.

She studied the expectant faces staring at her. She had noticed some small problems with the departments, but this was not the time. She would address those in private. Today she would try to motivate the group, gain their trust. "I have gathered you all here because you are the heartbeat of this casino. I know sometimes you feel like the ugly duckling, and the Palm Oasis gets all the attention. But I plan to turn this place into a swan. If you are anything like me, I am sure you have your own ideas on how to run your own department more efficiently. You just wish someone would listen to you. I am here to listen and more importantly to learn."

"Amen," shouted Deanna. "The cage could use some new equipment. The stuff we have is ancient. Everything is always breaking and slowing down the whole operation. The time difference between a machine count and a hand count is hours." All the money coming into the casino needed to be counted whether it was deposited in a slot machine or lost at the gaming tables.

Caroline smiled, pleased that this was an easy problem to fix. "I can do that. What could be more important than counting the money? Money makes our world go round."

Everyone laughed. She started taking notes in a spiral notebook. Everyone likes free stuff and since John had given her a blank check to modernize the casino, she intended to spend some money.

Joanna chimed in, "Can we have some better cameras? I want to make sure my assets are protected."

Tribal members were shareholders of the tribe. Not only did Joanna earn a salary, but all tribal members also received a remittance check every month. Belonging to certain Native American tribes was like winning the lottery, only better. The money just kept rolling in, and jobs were guaranteed for life.

For the next few hours Caroline listened patiently to all their concerns. Most people just wanted someone to listen to them. John had taught her that. He always listened to her with attention, which had given her so much confidence. By the time she adjourned the meeting, she left with a notebook full of ideas and suggestions, a pain in her head, and a bigger pain in her butt from sitting. To clear her head, she decided to take a walk through the casino to stretch out and schmooze with the customers on the floor.

Later, she was called to help Jesus pay out a $20,000 jackpot. He verified the machine hadn't been tampered with. The casino didn't give up that much money without a thorough check. After collecting the player's social security number, a jackpot of that size needed to be reported to the government, she escorted him to the cage where he retrieved a voucher for the cash. To make it all official, Jesus and Caroline posed with the young Marine. Soon there would be a picture of him on the winner's wall he could show to all his buddies.

A loud growl erupted from her stomach. In her old life she would never have forgotten to eat, but her job was so demanding food sometimes slipped her mind. Now her diet mostly consisted of hot dogs from the snack bar. Free food was another perk of the job, although she seldom found the time to eat a whole meal.

She took up her favorite watching position, leaning against a slot machine biting a stale hot dog, with a clear view of the roulette table in front of her. Watching was easier if she remained hidden. Dealers got nervous when they were being observed by the casino manager. They were used to being supervised from behind. There was always a boss standing in the pit. But they never expected to be watched from the casino floor.

A walking breathing kewpie doll stood across from her, a permanent grin plastered on her face. Suda wore big eyelashes and even bigger hair. Casino gossips told her the dealer's story. She had been a *kathoey*, commonly called a ladyboy, when she lived in Thailand. Ladyboys could be transgender women or effeminate gay males. Suda was transgender. After undergoing reassignment surgery, she immigrated to America. In Palm Springs, Halloween was like Homecoming for transgenders, but she had never seen anyone as fine boned and delicate as Suda.

She didn't care what she had been because she always greeted her with a hug, and in this no-touch politically correct corporate atmosphere, she appreciated a little human contact. Being around her always put a smile on Caroline's face. Every day she received the tip report of all casino employees. A pro at making money, Suda was always in the top five. She decided to settle back and watch her deal.

All croupiers preferred to deal their favorite games. When she dealt, Caroline took pride in her ability to deal roulette like a pro because it was one of the more difficult games to learn. To be skillful at the game, a dealer should be able to add quickly and accurately in order to calculate the payoffs, and most importantly great dexterity was needed to clear the layout and stack the chips. A tiny Suda peeked out from behind the roulette wheel, a beautiful piece of hardware carved out of polished mahogany, then varnished to a high gloss shine. She decided to test her skill retention, how fast she could calculate the winning payouts.

A solitary man sat at the roulette table, your average white, nondescript middle-aged male, the kind who thrived on the attention of a pretty female dealer like Suda. He kept sending admiring glances her way, enchantment written all over his face. His quick hands placed chips as fast as he could on the numbers on the layout. Once the layout was plastered with chips Suda placed the ball between her thumb and index finger, spun her wrist sending it on its way, whizzing around the wheel.

When the ball slowed down, she called out, "No more bets," and waved her hand across the table signaling the end of action. The ball fell into the slot for number twenty-eight. "Twenty-eight Black is a winner."

Caroline watched Suda carefully clear the losing chips around the winning number, next she picked the losing chips from the outside bets. She stood on her tippy toes as she gracefully swept the losing chips in a zigzag fashion collecting them in one pile. She deliberately leaned over the table in a shirt tailored so tightly her buttons strained at the fabric. Casino wisdom 101: tighter shirts, better tips. Her movements were art performed with a graceful choreography.

Caroline worked out the payout in her head, while Suda cleared the layout, assembled the payout, and used her left hand to push it out to the customer. Caroline studied the stack of chips and realized something didn't add up. The payout didn't match her calculations. Experience taught her not to walk over and alert the dealer about her mistake. Leaning closer into the slot machine, she continued to watch. One overpayment could be a mistake, any more than one and the dealer was stealing.

Out of the corner of one eye she spotted Jesus approaching her. If Suda saw anyone talking to her, it would blow her cover. As she caught his eyes, she held up her finger to her mouth, signaling for him to stay silent. He appeared befuddled at her motion but passed by as if she wasn't standing there.

After a few more spins Caroline reluctantly pulled out her cell phone and dialed surveillance. "Put all your cameras on table six, the roulette game. I'll be up in a minute."

From her watching spot, she searched the pit trying to locate the floor person. Instead of supervising the action on the games, she found him leaning on the podium, eyes focused upward to the television screen hanging from the ceiling, watching the Dodgers play.

Suddenly she lost her appetite. She threw the last bite of her hot dog into the trash. The Night Hawk was a "go for your own joint." All dealers kept their own tips, which meant they didn't have to split tips with the other dealers. Because they kept every chip they dropped down their tip box, their main focus became increasing those tips. Her heart broke just a little bit as she climbed the stairs to surveillance, a room so secret few people who worked in the casino were allowed to enter it.

Her destination was a small cubicle just outside the main surveillance room filled with monitors, and a desk reserved to review the tape from the roulette game. As Joanna tapped a few keys on the computer, a video of the roulette game, taken from overhead cameras, appeared on the monitor. She rewound the film, and together they studied the last half hour of play.

Caroline pointed at the spot on the tape where Suda pushed out the payment. "Zoom in. Let's review this payout. A chip has been placed on every split and corner, your standard picture bet, which pays one hundred chips." Picture bets were the common bets all dealers memorized in training class. "Next, five chips sit straight up on the number, which pays one hundred and seventy-five chips. I calculate one hundred for the picture bet and one hundred and seventy-five for the five straight ups, which adds up to a total of two hundred and seventy-five chips, or in this case dollars."

They watched her assemble the payout. Suda used her left hand to push out the money, one hundred seventy-five blue dollar chips, and two black one-hundred-dollar chips stacked on top. When he received the money, the player immediately threw two twenty-five-dollar chips in her direction

"See that? She passes the customer an extra hundred-dollar chip and then he tips her fifty dollars, two quarter chips. My guess, they are splitting the overpayment, working together. It infuriates me the way she giggles as she accepts the tip. It's almost like she's laughing at the ease of stealing Shotowa money."

After studying the next few spins, Joanna agreed.

"You're damn straight she's cheating. Watch how she overpays him, by one chip but it is always a hundred-dollar chip." The film kept rolling. The next payout should have been six hundred dollars, but the player got seven hundred. "What an elaborate way to steal. Why doesn't she drop some chips down her tip box when she thinks no one is looking?"

"Because it is always better to work with a partner. She overpays him and he hands her a tip which she drops into her box. If I hadn't noticed the payout was wrong, it would seem legit. If she got caught, her next move would be to bat those big brown eyes, and cry. 'I made a mistake.'" Caroline was very aware of the tag team method.

Joanna studied the screen and wrote down some notes. "I think we've got all the evidence we need here. I'll write up the report."

Caroline shook her head. "Hard to believe. They know they're on camera and that we have the ability to track their payouts for the last month. How could any rational person think they can get away with cheating? She's willing to lose her job for a few lousy tips?"

"That's what we think. But there are so many tables on the floor and the dealers know we aren't capable of watching everyone all the time. So they take their chances, stealing small bits of money," Joanna murmured. "When people work in the money store some of them begin to believe the money is theirs. Odds are, if you weren't watching her, she probably would have gotten away with it at least for today. I'm sure this isn't the first time she's cheated."

She shrugged both shoulders and sighed. "In surveillance, we try to catch cheaters, but even we can't see everything."

"Write up the report. Next, how should we discipline the floorman? Let's..." Caroline paused as she tried to decide what would be an appropriate punishment. "...write him up, final warning." Then she paused again for a second, decided against her first decision, and shook her head. "No. We have to fire him. If we are going to send a message, we have to really send an explicit message. We don't pay the supervisors to watch baseball. I have to call Derrick. Once I find out the player's name, let's make sure he gets banned. I'm sure he played a part in this scheme, her accomplice. It's less risky to overpay a player than to steal money straight from the rack. They're lucky we don't arrest them. Let's wrap this up quickly. I want Suda off this property today."

There were more opportunities for dealers to steal than any other casino employee. Dealers made hundreds of payouts an hour, handled thousands of dollars of cash a day, and there was only one floorman to supervise four tables. The money for all other departments had to be balanced, but it was impossible to keep track of the money at the table games. With so much cash passing through their hands, it wouldn't be hard for a dealer to push some bills up their sleeve. With twenty-five dollar chips the same size as the other chips, a dealer could just place a small value chip over a high value chip, then drop both in their tip box. A casino depended on the honesty of their employees, but as backup they positioned cameras everywhere. They lived by the philosophy, trust but verify.

Later that afternoon Brandon and Caroline silently stood beside Suda while she cleared out her locker.

Brandon handed her black plastic bags to store her belongings in. Once the locker was cleaned out, they escorted her down the employee-only corridor, past the security desk, and out the back door. Trying on her best remorseful face she pleaded, "I've never done this before. I so sorry. Please, one more chance."

Caroline wasn't sympathetic to her pity party. She had heard this song and seen this dance too many times. Employees from all the other departments begged to gain admission to dealing school. New dealers were so grateful when they first got hired. They could make hundreds a day, and if they possessed a healthy amount of charm, they could potentially earn over six figures a year. For some of them, no amount of money was enough. They couldn't resist the temptation to put their hand in the till. The one inflexible rule casinos abided by: anyone who gets caught stealing doesn't get a chance to steal a second time.

Suda's departure was perfectly timed, right before shift change, when the maximum number of dealers would witness her walk of shame. She wanted the message to sink in, there was a new lady boss in town, and if anyone cheated, they would be caught. When she left work that day, she felt like a bitch, but a bitch doing what she had to do. She wouldn't let anyone steal from the tribe. She had sworn to protect their assets.

Chapter Three

A Dealer Must Be Able to Concentrate in a Very Loud Environment

Ten minutes before each shift began, the dealers gathered in the employees-only hallway that led to the gaming floor. At their daily briefing they were updated about the goings on in the casino, after which they would receive their game assignments. Through the years Caroline modeled her interactions by trying to follow John's example.

His charisma and charm shone through when he spoke with both employees and customers. He remembered everyone's name, and because of this, people confided their problems to him and shared personal details about their family life. He didn't fake his feelings; he really cared. Because the employees felt a connection to John, they strived to do a better job. She wanted to follow his example, so in the last month she made getting to know her employees and their stories one of her top priorities.

One of the first things anyone who played at the Night Hawk noticed was the diversity of nationalities working there. A group of them now stood against the wall. She marveled once again at how interesting, brave, and sometimes horrifying their individual stories were. Standing to her right was Binh, a short, slightly balding man, who escaped Vietnam in a leaky boat. To her left, Kim's family had hidden in the jungle as they walked from Cambodia to Thailand before starting over in America. Next to her, Nadia, a Ukrainian bride, married an American she met on a dating website. Only later she learned he didn't own a house near the ocean only a shack at Lake Elsinore. Across from her, June, a gentle Scottish woman, made her way to America by winning the green card lottery sponsored by the Department of State. And most impressive of all, tiger mom, Ling, brought her family to the United States only five years ago, and now her daughter would be entering UCLA in the fall. There were many more dealers standing there, and Caroline's goal was to learn all their stories.

All of these people from across the globe and the fifty states somehow found themselves forty miles off the interstate slinging cards or pouring drinks in the High Desert. Since some of her dealers had lived under the most ruthless dictators on the planet, she figured they could handle the occasional aggressive customer with ease. Whether they came from a small village in Thailand or the capital of Ukraine, she was always amazed at how fast everyone assimilated into American culture. Her employees could tell her how to buy designer goods at the cheapest prices, recommend the most prestigious schools in the area or, most importantly, if she was ever in the market for a nip or tuck, they would steer her to the best plastic surgeons.

The majority of them got into the casino business because someone from their village or town attended dealing school, and once they started working, word spread like wildfire through the community that casinos were a great place for a person without official college credentials to get a well-paying job. She doubted if working here was their American dream but being here was helping them live the American dream. She considered them her band of vagabonds, but wasn't she a vagabond herself?

Usually they bantered with each other, in a variety of languages, but stony silence greeted her this morning. The dealers stayed suspiciously silent, apprehension written all over their faces, eyes pointed at the ground. Suda had been fired, and they all feared they would be next. She believed a little fear was a necessary thing, it kept people honest, but she also wanted her face of the house employees to have a positive and upbeat attitude. The juggling act of balancing the two was a tricky proposition.

Derrick introduced Caroline. "Our new manager has a few things she would like to share with you. Show her some respect, guys."

The dealers were her biggest critics. She needed to be honest with them or they would tune her out. You could pander to the customers, but the dealers could always spot a fake. She took a breath, inhaling the strong odor of conflicting perfumes mingling in the air. "Hi everybody, looking sharp in your new uniforms."

June spoke with a soft lilt. "These are a damn shite better than the last ones. The buttons kept popping off."

"That's because your shirts were so tight," the ever-blunt Nadia added. Her comment broke the tension in the corridor. Everyone laughed, including June.

As part of the upgrade, it had been decided that the casino needed a new start, and there seemed no better way to change things up and lift morale than by buying everyone new clothes. Today the dealers stood at attention in new, freshly pressed, black pants and white shirts, topped with a blue vest covered in a diamond pattern.

Caroline began her comments, in an upbeat tone. "It is my great pleasure to work with all of you. I just want to get to know you better so I can best address your needs. If I pass by you at a dead game and stop to ask some questions, don't be nervous. Also, feel free to share all your thoughts and concerns with me. I am instituting an open-door policy."

She paused for effect and then laid down the law. "One more thing, there is a zero-tolerance policy on cheating. If you see cheating and fail to report it, I consider that the same as you cheating. Don't worry, if you aren't doing anything wrong, you have nothing to fear. Now, feel free to bitch about me and all the changes we are making in the casino, but remember the break room is the place to complain. Say anything you want about me. I'm tough, I can take it. But if I ever hear any of you talking negatively about management or the tribe on the casino floor in front of the customers, you're history."

"You mean like Suda," Nadia finished everyone's thoughts.

"Let's just say she had addition problems." Caroline stared straight at the group to let the message sink in. "Now go out there and make some money."

Whenever possible, she tried to work in her private office with the door open because if she wanted to have an open-door policy, it was important that it physically remained open. Employees with a problem would be reluctant to knock if it was closed.

She glanced up from a status report to find Binh lingering in the hallway. Sensing he wanted to talk to her, she needed to figure out how to best coax him into her office. Trying to act casual but dying to find out what brought him to her, she leaned back in her swivel chair and nonchalantly gestured for him to sit in the chair in front of her desk. "Come in. Have a seat. Close the door behind you."

He took a seat but remained quiet as a blush began to cross his face, painting it red. The two sat in uncomfortable silence for a moment before she finally spoke. "I really want to hear what you have to say, Binh. You're a valued team member here."

They sat quietly for a minute more, but then as he began to open up, apprehension defined his body language. "It is Derrick. He always wants to borrow money. He says he will pay back, but he never has. Last night he asked me for money."

"How much are we talking about?"

"Five hundred dollars sometimes. Once, a thousand dollars. Now he wants five hundred. I don't have extra money. My daughter is in college, much bills."

Panic bells rang in her head. You couldn't stop employees from buying gifts for their bosses, but this was over the limit. No employee was allowed to accept a gift of over fifty dollars, and they were never allowed to borrow money from another employee, or a customer, or lend them money.

"Does he just borrow from only you, or does he borrow from the other dealers, too?"

"Some, if he thinks they will not say no."

"Why don't you just say no? He can't make you give him money."

Binh squirmed in his seat. "If you do not give him money, he assigns you bad game and you no make money."

She sympathized. The majority of a dealer's income came from tips and being assigned to bad games could cost a dealer hundreds of dollars a day. "I promise I will do everything I can to get your money back. A shakedown like this will not be tolerated. You didn't escape to America to be threatened by an Irish asshole. Remember our conversation here remains confidential." An employee never wanted to get the reputation of being a snitch.

As soon as Binh left her office she summoned John to the Night Hawk. The allegations needed to be investigated before they could decide on the appropriate punishment, and she wanted his counsel. Thankfully, Thursday was Derrick's day off, which meant they could question all the dealers without his knowledge.

John decided Nadia could be easily coaxed into telling them what was happening downstairs. She strolled into the room like she owned the casino. He put his arm around her, easing her into a chair. Once she was comfortable, he pulled up a chair beside her. From her position at her desk Caroline decided to observe the master perform his magic.

He stared into Nadia's eyes concentrating his full attention on them. Anyone would have imagined he was in love with her. "Nadia, you look so gorgeous today."

By a certain age a person wore the face they could afford, and apparently Nadia could afford eyelash extensions, plump lips, sculpted cheeks, a pointed chin, and new breasts inserted to replace the old pair. All of her disposable income was spent on plastic surgery. On her breaks she loved to pose in the back booth snapping away, posting selfies of herself on social media. John had been smart to appeal to her vanity.

John's usual soft tone switched to serious. "We need to know, has Derrick ever tried to borrow money from you?"

Indignant, Nadia puffed out her ample chest, tossed back her luscious mane of long auburn hair, and snorted. "He tried, but my money is my money. I keep for myself. Not even my husband touches it. Derrick is an idiot." She emphasized the word idiot pronouncing it slowly, dragging it out.

"Well I know you are smarter than most of us. But the others, does he hit them up for loans?"

"The new ones, the ones who don't speak good English. If they don't give him money, it's *pai-gow* all day. We make no tips on that horrible game. He knows if he did that to me, I would be straight up here complaining."

Pai-gow was an ancient Chinese game notorious for attracting people who didn't tip. It was a slow game because most hands ended in a tie.

While Nadia filled them in on the details of Derrick's extortion scheme Caroline took notes. Not for the first time since moving into management, she felt like a detective in a crime novel.

"Nadia, you have been such a great help." John held her hands as he led her from the room. "We want to protect our dealers and make it impossible for anyone to shake them down for money. You're perceptive, I don't need to tell you what is said here, stays here." He held her gaze again.

Everything they talked about would be spread around the break room in less than an hour, but Caroline figured the gossip would cause other dealers to reach out to them. After the meeting, they began to call the dealers into the office, one by one, to ask about Derrick. Once they realized she and John were aware of Derrick's scheme, the dealers seemed relieved the secret was out.

She spent the afternoon compiling a list of the names and the amount Derrick owed them. At the end of the day, she tabulated the numbers on her computer. Holding up a printout containing names of dealers, she read out the totals to John. "I am sorry to report Derrick has borrowed over twenty thousand dollars from the dealers, an amazing amount of money. The nerve of that bastard! Firing him isn't enough. Please can we throw him in jail?" All of her life she had been told how prevalent white-collar crime was, but this was certainly a novel way to steal money.

John apologized. "Sorry to break the bad news, I already checked with the gaming people. Since he was borrowing money, technically no crime has been committed. But the tribe will do everything we can to recover the money, although he probably lost most of it. My sources at the casino in Hemet tell me Derrick has been seen throwing down thousands in bets at the craps games there. I hope he enjoyed his gambling spree. Our only legal recourse is to fire him."

Furious, Caroline hit back. "While you're at it, make sure he gets banned from every casino in America."

A mischievous gleam appeared in John's eyes. "First we have to catch him red-handed. Get Binh back upstairs. I have an idea."

****

The next day, all the pieces were set in place for the sting. In the surveillance room, Caroline and John were joined by Brandon and Joanna as they sat at a table. A surge of excitement ran through her body, like a private detective on a stakeout.

With eyes riveted to the computer screen, they followed the action being filmed by a camera which had been rotated to the best position to observe Binh's open locker, situated on a long, lonely 'employee only' corridor behind the restaurant. Earlier, Binh had texted Derrick to meet him ten minutes before the start of the shift. As Derrick walked up to meet him, his beady eyes darted from right to left, scanning the corridor.

Slowly Binh pulled out one bill from his wallet, exposing it to the camera, one hundred dollars. Watching him on the monitor, Caroline saw his hands shaking. After the first bill he kept pulling out money until he placed five hundred dollars into Derrick's waiting hand. The cash had been provided by the casino on the off-chance Derrick refused to give it back.

Derrick tilted his head to Binh and nodded. They couldn't hear his comments, but he must have been satisfied because he put the money in his pocket and walked away. Up in the surveillance room as high fives were shared across the table, Caroline experienced a sense of triumph in the way her team bonded together to thwart a crooked manager.

"This one thinks he's so damn smart with his skinny suits and his snotty little accent." Joanna imitated Derrick's accent. "Top of the morning to you, Mr. Donegal."

"I know he likes to butter everybody up but now he is toast," Caroline added.

Another day, another walk of shame, another employee out the door. She was getting used to this. John and Brandon smiled at each other and shouted, "Another one bites the dust!" Anyone could see the bond between the two men ran deep.

They threw fake punches in the air. "We've still got it. Just like in high school in Palm Springs. Brandon and I would kick the crap out of anyone who made fun of Native Americans or African Americans. We scored one point for kicking the butt of a white kid, two if their parents were celebrities. Brandon always won, none of the kids in school could kick his ass. We even joined the Marines together. To insult us, the whites called us Caramel and Chocolate. I think you can figure out who was who."

Caroline laughed. "My two favorite foods."

Brandon seemed almost stricken by the words coming out of John's mouth. "Don't get the wrong idea, Ms. Popov. We never went looking for any trouble, but we never turned away from it either."

Caroline and John entered the employee lounge together as a team ready to confront Derrick. Casinos are careful to handle their problems behind closed doors, far away from the eyes of the public. Searching the room, they spied him comfortably ensconced in a booth, taking a huge bite out of his hamburger.

John slid next to Derrick, boxing him in. Caroline took a place across from the men. "I don't mean to disturb your lunch." John winked at her. "Who am I kidding, I am getting such a kick out of this. We caught you extorting money from the dealers. I'm just sorry this isn't the old Mafia days, when we could just take a problem employee out back and beat them to a bloody pulp. But Caroline says we have to do things the corporate way, with documentation. Fortunately, we have all the evidence we need on tape. Derrick, maybe you can enlighten me, why does everybody always forget about the cameras?"

Derrick's attitude turned defiant. "Those were gifts given freely."

"What a pathetic defense. So, you never borrowed money. It really makes no difference, either way, you are no longer employed here. A man of your intelligence doesn't forget you are only allowed to accept gifts of fifty dollars or less." She had double checked the employee handbook last night to verify her facts. Suddenly ravenous, she reached her hand over the table liberating a French fry from his plate. "I think I'll borrow this. You won't be eating it. See you in court."

She tilted her head. This was the signal Brandon and his assistant, Hector Deere, were waiting for. Hector was a shorter, wiry ex-Marine, but she was sure between the two of them they would get the job done. In unison, the men rose from their seats at the counter and stood in front of Derrick, blocking him from making an exit.

"For your convenience," John said sarcastically. "These guys are here to help you clean out your locker."

After Derrick was escorted to the other side of the employee entrance and safely deposited on the pavement, he spun to face her as she stood in the doorway. Expecting some major drama, employees smoking on the patio gleefully followed his unexpected departure. His face filled with such intense fury that she involuntarily flinched and stepped back.

Calmly enunciating each word clearly so everyone in the vicinity got a good show, he shouted, "I'll see you dead, you fucking bitch!"

Brandon flexed his muscle. "One more word from you and you won't be driving home in your car but will be leaving here in a police cruiser. Come on, make our day. We have nothing better to do."

She lost count years ago of the many threats which had been directed at her, although she no longer made security escort her to her car after work. She could never decide if she was overreacting or under-reacting, but she realized it wasn't normal to go to work and have people say they were going to kill you, out loud in front of witnesses. Derrick wasn't the first, and he wouldn't be the last, but was he crazy enough to kill her? She tried to shrug her worries off, get on with her day, but somewhere in the back of her mind the threat lingered because it only took one.

Chapter Four

A Dealer Must Be Able to Handle Difficult Customers in a Hostile Environment

A few days later, after a surprise rainstorm, the landscape erupted in wildflowers. Indian paintbrush, ocotillo, and purple mat along with a score of other blooms painted the desert floor in all shades of the rainbow. Caroline gazed out the window, admiring the countryside as she drove down the hill past the gun range, around the corner, and onto the road leading to the casino. Her car meandered down the nearly empty highway of the High Desert, on her way to work, slowly enough to enjoy the glorious day. Stopping at the local donut shop, she took her time choosing a wide variety of tasty treats for the staff. Small gestures like bringing donuts were always a big hit in the employee lounge.

Back on the road, her eyes followed the arc of a bald eagle flying across the brilliant blue sky. The eagle landed on the far-left corner of the Night Hawk billboard, which stood above the road, fourteen feet high and forty-eight feet wide, enticing travelers to eat, play, win!

Glancing upward she did a double take. A new message painted bright red and ten feet high covered the billboard. '*Caroline Popov must die!*'

She slammed on the brakes, pulled to the curb and slammed the gear shift into park. She wanted to make sure she had read it right.

Getting out of the car she stood transfixed by the sign. Suddenly, her heart was pounding out of her chest, sure she was going to die. Her legs lost all sensation. Paralyzed, she collapsed to the ground, reeling from a panic attack. Somebody wanted her dead.

Derrick? Suda? Other people she had fired? A customer? Or someone who didn't want her to succeed in her job? What if someone who felt they deserved the job and were trying to run her down from the mountain and back to Palm Springs like a scared little girl?

She could never let them, her or him, know they had gotten to her. Just like the British public in World War II, she would keep calm and carry on because this was war. Most threats just rolled off her back. But painting one on a billboard changed a spur of the moment curse into a premeditated crime. She hated when horrible things happened on beautiful days.

Screw them. Caroline Popov was a force to be reckoned with.

Breathing in the early morning perfume of the flowering desert, a pleasant musky smell, she pulled out her cell phone and called the billboard company to have the sign replaced. Even if the sign hadn't spooked her, the message could put off some of the players. Experiencing an adrenaline high, on the ride to work her mood shifted between elation and panic.

Hector met her at her parking space. "I have been assigned to protect you today, Ms. Popov. We are all very concerned for your safety. We have also staffed more guards at all of the entrances."

"It's not necessary," she responded while a little voice inside her head told her, *Maybe it is.*

"Sorry, ma'am, but we all saw the billboard on the way to work. I'm just following the Chairman's orders."

"I know better than to argue with John. Here, help me with the donuts." She loaded up his arms with boxes. "Let's take these to the lounge."

When she entered the employee cafeteria, she caught an undercurrent of gossip permeating the atmosphere. Everyone was talking about the billboard. Since there was only one highway, really just a two-lane road running across the High Desert, ninety-nine percent of the employees had passed the sign on their way to work.

Her personal guard placed the donuts on a counter near the front door of the lounge making sure the boxes would be visible to everyone who entered the room. She plucked a coffee roll out of a box, and took it to a booth, her shadow following beside her. "For heaven's sake, grab a donut and come join me. This isn't a movie."

Her cell phone rang. "Caroline, I want you to stay in the hotel for the next few weeks until we know you are safe."

Detecting a note of panic in John's voice, she said, "This is just someone trying to get under my skin. If someone meant to kill me, they wouldn't announce their intention to the world."

"Whom do you think this someone could be?"

"Suda, Derrick, anyone who has lost money here, or any of the many people who've been fired from the Night Hawk. You aren't taking this seriously, are you?"

"In the past, probably not. But in the last few years the world has gone mad. Promise me you will be careful, and if you suspect anyone, you'll let me know."

"*Anyone*? I suspect everyone."

"You could be right. You know what they say, if you don't have enemies, you aren't doing a good job. Because I am responsible for your safety, so I can sleep at night, I will notify tribal security and the local police to keep tabs on your cabin. You have to let Brandon know before you leave for the night. He lives down the road from you. I want him to follow you home."

When she finally decided her day was over, she picked up her cell phone to call Brandon and noticed a new text message had appeared.

—*Hear you are having a bad day.*—

Well, they've got that right. She searched the text for the sender's identity, but the only salutation read— *your biggest fan.*—

The sender didn't leave a clue. She checked for a name, but only a local number was displayed. She googled the number, but found the owner was unknown.

Well, what a clever way to get my attention, wonder what they are trying to sell? Then she called Brandon because she had to admit, as much as she pretended not to be worried about the billboard, she would feel better knowing he was following her home.

****

Caroline tried to present a calm demeanor, but many of her employees had worked themselves up into quite a tizzy. Rumors circulated at high speed throughout the casino. Employees felt vulnerable when they left the building, asking security to escort them to their cars. Gaming decided now was a good time to face the issue straight on. It was time for active shooter training.

The many years of Brandon's military training and discipline were on display as he addressed the casino employees. "I know you are all freaked out about the billboard threatening Ms. Popov, but you need to know ninety-nine percent of threats are all talk, no action. As you can see, she is alive and well, sitting right beside me. We are investigating, but you are all aware how many thousands of people pass through this casino every week and some of them leave pissed off."

The room twittered in nervous laughter.

"Although in all probability this isn't serious, we need to remember the Night Hawk has to remain vigilant. To the outsider we might appear to be a sleepy casino, far from the glitz and glamour of Vegas, but active shooters shoot in all kinds of places for all kinds of reasons. We are located just down the road from the biggest Marine base in the world. It would be almost impossible for a terrorist to attack the base, but we are close by. We are a soft target. Hitting us would send a message. The high school down the road and the Night Hawk have the largest concentration of people all gathered in one place in this valley. Essentially a casino floor is one big room. All a shooter has to do is get through the front door and it's open season on us all."

Caroline realized how easy that would be, since there were no metal detectors at the doors.

More nervous laughter erupted in the room. Employees from all departments sat at tables dotting the showroom, filling in for a classroom. She scanned the room and observed a hundred pairs of eyes focused on the speaker. During most other classes the bored staff couldn't wait for the lecture to be over, as the speaker droned on about gambling addiction, sexual harassment, or alcohol awareness.

But in here, all ears paid attention to Brandon's words. Even before the billboard incident, there wasn't a person in the training room who hadn't contemplated horrendous scenarios, especially after the shooter at a Las Vegas casino picked off members of the audience at a country music concert—fifty-eight dead, four hundred eighty-nine wounded. The shooting hadn't surprised her.

Truth be told, she wondered why a domestic terrorist attack hadn't happened sooner. But even a massacre wouldn't keep customers away from the casinos.

Using a laser pointer, Brandon focused on the blueprint of the building. "Memorize all the exits. They have been marked in red. If you see or hear an active shooter, your first instinct should be to get away as fast as you can. Run as far from the casino as your feet will carry you. But if you can't run, hide. Find a room and lock the door. Hide under a table. Be very quiet and make sure you turn off your electronic devices."

He paused to emphasize his words. "If your cell phone rings, the noise might just alert the shooter to your position. Remember, active shooters don't negotiate. They kill as many people as possible. Don't make yourself an easy target. I can't promise you nothing will ever happen at the Night Hawk. But I can promise you my department is dedicated to your safety. I personally would take a bullet to keep anyone who works at the Night Hawk safe."

Taking the pulse of the room, Caroline realized the training really wasn't giving anyone reassurance. But the truth was there were no instructions for combating an active shooter. They didn't follow any rules. She was grateful because the casino staffed a highly trained security department who at least had a fighting chance to take down a shooter.

Chapter Five

Dealers Learn to Dummy Up and Deal, Never Confront a Customer

Driving home after a movie screening John wondered if he should relocate from Palm Springs to the High Desert and concentrate on the Night Hawk. The billboard incident had him spooked. He worried about Caroline because of the fifty miles separating them. All his employees were special, but he had a soft spot for her. When his cell phone rang, John pushed a button on the dashboard to use the hands-free option. "Yes, my queen?"

Her pleasant voice filled the car. "Just letting you know I'm home. When can I stop checking in every night?"

"When we find out who wants you dead." Question asked and answered.

"Moving on," she said. "Are you home yet, or still charming them at the Steak House?"

"For your information, I went to a screening at the Noir Film Festival tonight."

She sighed. "I miss that festival. It was my favorite. Remember the movie we attended last year? A classic, *Death Will Do You In.*"

"Who doesn't love a gritty crime drama in black and white starring a wisecracking private investigator working on an unsolved murder?"

She interrupted him. "Bantering snappy double entendres with a classy dame."

He added. "Intricate plots filled with double crosses, mistaken identity, and a few red herrings thrown in for fun. The best part, no special effects, the film making was pure. If an actor couldn't do it in real life, it wasn't on the screen."

"The fifties, a simpler time," she said wistfully.

Grateful that she was safe, he said, "Right now, I am driving to my mid-century house. I'll let you go, get some sleep. Thanks for calling."

"Thanks for caring." She hung up the phone.

His mind wandered back to when he had met his third wife at the gala for the Noir Festival. One of his main jobs as tribal chairman was to be an ambassador for the tribe. The Shotowa sponsored many of the major events in town, including the many film festivals. He marveled at how many different directions his job took him. His business degree really helped him plan and expand the business. But business etiquette was the most useful course he ever took.

He learned how to compose a business letter, write a resume, interview for a job, and the most helpful part, how to handle himself at a conference or charity event. Over a meal at a formal restaurant his professor taught him how to choose the right fork, who knew they called it cutlery, pass the food, carry on a conversation over dinner, and most importantly when to listen. Good manners and money turned out to be a great equalizer in Palm Springs society.

He had been standing at the bar when he spotted a vision on the stool next to him, like a goddess who had just stepped off the screen, her platinum blonde hair in a bouffant style, which highlighted her emerald-green eyes. Her long silk cocktail dress, curved in all the right places. He liked something to hold on to. The true epitome of a classy dame.

He smiled, handed her his card, the old tried and true approach. "Do you mind if I ask you a question? What do you think of our film festival, and can I buy you a drink while you give me the answer?"

From the recesses of her clutch, she pulled out her card.

He read it out loud, "Vanessa Taylor, Interior Designer," he paused. "Vanessa Taylor, I happen to be in need of your services. I just bought an original mid-century house, in the Twin Palms neighborhood. The only problem is that it hasn't been updated since the middle of the last century."

She raised her eyebrows. "Really."

He couldn't tell if she was exasperated or intrigued. He hired her and then he married her. She rose to the challenge and designed a house he was proud of in a neighborhood filled with mid-century moderns, the ultimate status symbol in Palm Springs. But she got tired of sitting in it alone every night while he was schmoozing strangers at the casino. Now, since he had sworn off marriage, he lived alone. He missed Vanessa but he wished he missed her more. He questioned if he was capable of feeling true love and making it last.

When he caught sight of the butterfly roof, he was home. Pulling into the driveway, lights erupted from the yard illuminating tall palm trees swaying in the gentle breeze. John punched a code in a pad opening the front door. Once inside he flipped the top switch on the wall, and in a few seconds the sultry voice of Frank Sinatra wafted throughout the house. He hated being alone in a silent house. The music set the mood for the wow factor. Another switch lit up a crystal chandelier revealing a huge butter leather sectional sofa, the focal point of the sunken living room.

On his way to the bedroom his ears pricked up, sensing an intruder. His tracking skills alerted him to someone in the back yard. Silently he began to retrace his steps ready to slink out through the front door. Now that Palm Springs had been rediscovered by affluent Angelenos, many who bought second homes in town, there was something to steal, and burglaries were on the rise in town. The cowboys always won because they had guns. In no mood to confront an intruder with a gun, he decided to sneak out and retreat down the street to call tribal security.

Just as he opened the front door, a voice shouted, "Dad, where are you going?" He spun around to catch a glimpse of his son, Kevin, passing through the open sliding glass door into the living room, a wet towel wrapped around him. Startled at how much his teenage son resembled him in his younger years, John worried at how much Kevin acted like the teenage John.

Relieved, he asked, "What are you doing here? Does your mother know where you are?" Kevin's mother was a high school sweetheart and tribal member. They'd reconnected after he left the Marines, but the connection quickly frayed.

Kevin walked over and gave him a hug. "Sure, I just wanted to come visit my dad."

"You caught me by surprise, of course I love having you here."

His son was the reason John couldn't move to the High Desert. He only had a few more years hopefully before Kevin went to college. He wanted to be available in case he wanted to spend time with him. "Let's not let this night go to waste, I'll order a pizza."

Chapter Six

British Dealers Are the Gold Standard

Derrick Thomas reclined on his Tartan couch, Guinness in hand, watching the telly.

I showed that bitch, let's see how well she sleeps tonight.

He couldn't quite pinpoint when the idea to deface the billboard occurred to him. Maybe it was triggered by the can of paint and ladder that had sat in his car for months. He'd meant to paint his bedroom, but due to his natural lethargy it never made it out of the trunk. To tell the truth, since *the bitch* arrived and fucked everything up, he didn't think he'd stick around long, much less make home improvements. But the job search had stalled, giving him plenty of time to plan a perfect act of revenge.

In the middle of the night, he climbed up the billboard, paint can in hand. He couldn't believe no one stopped him. Exhilarated, he hastily composed his masterpiece and slapped the paint on as fast as he could load up the brush. He had to get it done quickly and get out of there.

Totally indignant, he couldn't understand why he had gotten axed from working at the Night Hawk, the sweetest gig he had ever scored. They supplied him with an adequate salary, but the perks proved even better. Who could fault him if the dealers passed him a bit of cash for the best game assignments? What was the big deal about their sharing the wealth with management?

Employees weren't permitted to solicit funds, but the casino turned a blind eye when someone's frigging kid was pushing candy, or gift wrap for a school trip. He had just been soliciting a bit on the side for his special cause, a holiday at the poker tables. He wasn't a dosser, cheating or stealing from the casino. At his old places of employment, bribing the boss was standard practice. What did she know about paying her dues? Uppity bitch with her fancy degree, most likely the slag snagged the promotion by shagging the chairman.

Truth be told, he'd never lived in Ireland. His parents had immigrated to England when he was but a bun in the oven. The family resided on the mean streets of the East End, a borough of London popular with Irish immigrants. He had relatives who hailed from Donegal, and an Irish accent proved popular in the States, so he transformed himself into Derrick from Donegal.

He grew up playing cards and had been skilled at Twenty-Five, the national card game of Ireland. When he saw a billboard advertising a dealer training school, he applied straightaway. An inside job seemed a damn site warmer than bricking up council houses. The first game they taught him was roulette, the hardest game, which broke most of the trainees. After passing a head splitting training course, he had graduated to spinning the wheel in a casino. He proved himself to be nimble with his fingers and quick with the numbers.

For a few years he stayed in London, long enough

to gain competency in roulette, blackjack, and craps. Then he booked with an agency to join the growing band of itinerant British croupiers who supplied the world with gaming personnel.

His first stop had been South Africa where a white man lived a life of relative luxury compared to the native population. He worked in the Sun City casino outside of Johannesburg, the scariest frigging place in the world. His short tenure in management was disrupted by another fucking bitch, a woman named Sarah who caught him diverting a few bills from the drop box into his pocket before they could be counted.

"Please, Sarah," he'd pleaded, "Give me another frigging chance."

Her response was to have casino security guards rough him up and throw him into a dark, dank cell where he slept for a night before they deported him from the country. A night in jail taught him a valuable lesson: never steal from a casino; they meant frigging business.

In those days the world was wide, and jobs were plentiful. A buddy from his London days secured employment for him at a new joint opening in Panama. Once again, he rose quickly through the ranks, but at the end of the year his buddy, the casino manager, was relieved of his position. Derrick followed him to his next job in Costa Rica. For the next decade he crisscrossed the world from the warm sands of Namibia to the cold streets of The Czech Republic. Casino jobs were plentiful but hardly permanent. His wanderlust took him to water. He worked at small casinos on riverboats and then on to mega cruise ships.

While working on the Regal Star as a casino

manger he met his future wife, a nurse from San Diego who came with an impressive dowry, a green card. She fancied a man in a suit, and he fancied settling down in America. The brief and turbulent marriage ended when his bride discovered he had depleted their bank account at roulette tables in Temecula. He always prided himself on his gift of gab, but he couldn't convince her that he was just on a bad run, and his fortunes would soon turn around. She bitched at him so hard he thought his head would explode. Just to make her stop talking he punched her in the face. He got a job in the desert to get away from that bitch after she threatened to take out a restraining order against him. Screw all those bitches; he was done with them.

It was one thing to be fired, but to be shown the door in front of the whole casino was not on. It was another bitch's trademark move. Caroline got a hard-on from escorting him off the premises as the shift was changing, mortifying him in front of his peers. Never showed anyone respect, always trying to prove a point. She got off on humiliating him in front of two shifts.

Yeah, he did shout out, "This isn't the last you've seen of me you fucking bitch," as he was deposited on the sidewalk, but who could blame him? She was melting his head.

His anger grew, feeding on itself, he picked up the remote and kept hitting the back button, replaying the scene of the police discovering the billboard. Every time they walked over to the sign, he paused the action and screamed, "Caroline Popov must die!"

It was brilliant, fucking brilliant, and then he let out a huge Guinness burp.

Chapter Seven

A "Whale" Is a High Roller. A "George" Is a Big Tipper

Navigating through the casino on a Saturday night was liking swimming in a shoal of fish. A shoal differed from a school because all the fish swam in different directions from each other. Like fish, casino patrons stay together for social reasons. Bobbing and weaving through the crowded gaming floor, making her way toward the bar, Caroline swerved to avoid running into a customer, and almost collided with a cocktail waitress who carried a tray loaded with drinks. With Saturdays being the most stressful night of the week, it was important to be present to support her employees and greet customers. Filled to capacity, every slot machine seat occupied, and the bar standing room only, energy vibrated from the place.

She wrinkled her nose at the air thick with smoke, as she picked up empty glasses and ashtrays littered with cigarette butts. A disc jockey pumped loud music through the air, creating a party atmosphere designed to increase alcohol intake and loosen wallets.

As she leaned over the crowded bar to deposit the empty drink glasses on the counter, to her delight she spotted her favorite player from down the hill in Palm Springs, someone she genuinely liked. Ray Gordon, a slight man with dirty-blond hair, perched on a stool, precariously holding his long-stemmed tumbler of Beaujolais, his favorite wine, which looked like it was too big for him. His face trended young from a distance, but close up she saw the years of wine drinking in the splotches of red written over his pale skin. He had been one of her first customers on her first night dealing—then countless more times throughout the years. Walking up to him she threw her arms around him and pecked him on the cheek.

He leaned into her greeting. "I missed seeing your pretty face, so I took a drive up the hill to visit my favorite boss. You left so fast I didn't have a chance to congratulate you on your promotion. I can't seem to win anything since you've transferred to the Night Hawk. Now that I've found my lucky charm again, do your magic."

"Here give me your hands." She placed his soft hands in hers and rubbed them, their tradition. "I just rubbed some luck on you." As much as she would have liked to believe he made the drive just to see her, she suspected there was also an ulterior motive for his surprise appearance at the Night Hawk—chasing the money.

Figuring out customers' motives was impossible because they were a finicky lot. They might play at a casino because they liked the manager, or it was close to their house, or perhaps the casino was giving away a gift or having a drawing. Mostly, they returned to a place because they sincerely believed they could win there, or conversely, if they played at another casino they were destined to lose. But alliances could change quickly. When she had worked at the Night Hawk's sister casino in Palm Springs, she hoped her customers were loyal to the Palm Oasis, but when she left to work at the Night Hawk, she found many of the same customers also playing there.

Since both casinos were owned by the Shotowa Tribe, points accumulated at one location could be redeemed at the other. The casino business was all about the points, the perks, the comps—gifts, food, or rooms—basically anything the customers could get for free. However, *free* was a term of grand delusion. You had to lose a whole lot of money before the casino gave a customer anything for free.

"I don't see your better half, where is he?" she inquired. "Hiding at his favorite slot machine?"

"Robert had to attend a chamber of commerce charity event tonight. Ever since he got elected to city council, he's too busy to come out and play with me. Did you know, since the last election the entire city council in Palm Springs is gay?"

Like forty percent of Palm Springs' population, Ray was gay. Caroline loved her gays. She wished everyone could live in Palm Springs, even if only for a year, to experience how the diverse group of people who called the city home lived and worked in harmony. Working in such a tolerant environment had dramatically increased her understanding of the world. It didn't mean everyone got along. It wasn't a utopia, some people got on each other's nerves. People were just people. Some of them were annoying, but their temperament had nothing to do with their race, nationality, or sexual orientation.

The casino books would be in the black tonight, Ray was her favorite player, but that didn't make him a smart player. He relied on intuition, not rules. Any real gambler could tell you, the quickest way to lose was to rely on feelings. The only way to win was to utilize basic strategy when playing, and even then, the odds still favored the house.

But he wasn't a problem gambler. He played for entertainment, not money. Like social drinkers, or social smokers, social gamblers also existed. He maintained his even temperament no matter how much he lost. With fondness she recalled the first time she had dealt to him. Watching his pile of chips slowly disappearing into her rack, in sympathy she would apologize. "You must hate me. I'm taking all your money."

"Nonsense, I love coming here. Where else can I chat with lovely dealers, drink my wine, and escape from my responsibilities for a few hours. People might think I'm crazy, but everyone has to have a hobby. Win or lose, nothing makes me happier than a night at the blackjack table. Playing cards certainly beats a night at the opera." For the first time standing behind a table the weight of taking people's money on her chest lessened.

Of course, people who said it's only money usually had plenty of it. Over the years she had learned losing meant different things to different people. Ray was a very successful television producer, some of his shows were still running and some played in reruns, but they all had one thing in common, they sent him a check every month. His wealth was so great he could lose thousands, and it would be a drop in the bucket of his net worth.

"Would you like to play your usual limit?" He nodded. "Let me make a call."

A few minutes later she escorted Ray to a table with a *RESERVED* sign prominently displayed on the layout. What a whale—a huge player, bought with his money was special treatment. Like all high rollers Ray loved having his own blackjack table, which elevated him to a special category above all the other players. The minimum bet at the table was one hundred dollars and the maximum was $10,000. He handed the dealer a thick stack of cash.

Ling carefully laid out the one-hundred-dollar bills in four columns of five, front sides facing up on the green felt of the table layout. Then she turned the bills over-exposing the back side making it visible to the overhead cameras. She announced the total. The pit boss counted the cash with his eyes, then nodded his approval. Every step carefully verified. No one wanted to make a mistake counting such a large amount of money. Handing out the wrong amount of chips could result in instant termination. The dealer passed out rows of chips to Ray—ten one-thousand-dollar chips, ten five-hundred-dollar chips, two stacks of hundred-dollar chips, and two stacks of twenty-five-dollar chips, totaling $20,000 worth of ceramic chips.

Ray reached across the table to grab his chips but his elbow got in the way and knocked over his glass of wine, spilling his Beaujolais right onto the Ben Franklins, soaking them in red wine.

"I'm so sorry," a mortified Ray apologized, as Caroline and the dealer patted the money, drying it with towels stored under the table specifically for this purpose.

"Are you kidding, wet money plays the same as dry money. I'm just so glad you came to visit us." Then she rubbed his hands one last time.

He would lose thousands in one night, and it killed her. There were so many nights in the early days when she was so deeply in debt, she had wanted to scream, "Just give me the money. You're going to lose it anyway." She had worked so hard, only to eventually lose her money and property, she couldn't believe rich people could be so glib.

The glass chandelier hanging over the pit began to sway, followed by a rumbling in the background. The lights flickered. "Lids up," she shouted.

All action at the tables stopped. In unison the dealers retrieved the lids for the games from their storage place under the table and placed them over the rack of chips. The dull roar of the casino morphed into silence, everyone terrified that this was the big one.

The money must be protected if the power failed. The room shook, accompanied by the crackle of glass breaking in the distance. The shaking continued for thirty more seconds and then abruptly stopped. Everyone stood still, waiting, and in a few seconds the room shook again, an aftershock. Then as quickly as it began—it was over, another earthquake in the desert. The dealers replaced their lids back in their places. Broken glass would be swept up, and everyone returned to their play, happy it wasn't the big one.

As the night wore on, Ray had lost his original buy-in and requested a $20,000 marker. While he played the shift changed. At two a.m., a heavy cart rolled out onto the crowded casino, flanked on either side by Hector and Brandon, guarding it every step of the way. The most important job of the security department was to oversee the box pull. Security guards removed drop boxes filled with thousands of dollars of cash from the table replacing them with new empty boxes. They placed the filled boxes inside large metal cages inside the carts, to secure them as they made their journey through the gaming floor to the count room.

Ray lost eighty thousand dollars that night but not all of the money would translate to casino profit. Dealers loved him because he was a 'George,' a great tipper. A large portion of his money wouldn't go into the casino's drop boxes but would find its way into dealers' tip boxes. Even subtracting for the tips, she was pretty sure the Night Hawk would record its best hold since she had arrived. It was called *the hold* because it was held by the casino, the difference between the amount of money the customers put in the drop box and the amount they left the casino with minus dealer tips. The hold was the house win. Casinos not only had a built-in advantage, but it was supported by a very large bank. Most of the time the customer would run out of money before the house did.

Native American nations were sovereign countries, the casino bank their Treasury, casino chips the currency. The count room kept track of the trade surplus, and there was always a surplus. The room was not visible from the casino floor—hidden behind the cashier's cage in a very nondescript place. But looks can be deceiving because it was the most heavily surveilled room in the casino. A room filled with unmarked bills in every denomination could be a real temptation to thieves. Only a select few were allowed in there, and they had to pass through two doors to gain entrance.

Nervously, Caroline waited at the first door for

surveillance to buzz her in. Hearing a loud buzz, she opened the door, and immediately the heavy door slammed shut imprisoning her in a narrow long corridor flanked on either side with shelves. Nothing could be taken into the count room, no exceptions. She deposited her personal possessions on the shelves, which were filled with the belongings of the people already working inside. While in the room she would have no access to her cell phone or notebook. Outside the door of the room where the money was counted, she had to wait for surveillance to buzz her in again.

Walking in, she waved to the count ladies, not wanting to distract them from their job. A group of middle-aged women, their hair sprinkled with gray, gathered around a long square table, piles of cash spread out before them. The casino had learned that if you needed great caches of cash counted out, it was better to trust the job to people with families. Call it sexism, backed up by statistics, the tribe believed women were more honest.

Hector placed a metal box with two locks before each of the women. Some boxes were open, some waited to be unlocked. Hector traveled from lady to lady, opening the top lock with one key while Paula, the count room manager, opened the bottom lock. The double security made it harder for greedy hands to pick the casino's pocket. Harder but not impossible, because when there is money involved, people always manage to find a way.

"Who has box one hundred three?" Caroline inquired.

A petite Chinese woman named Sandy, raised a hand. "Me."

"You might find the cash a little sticky. The customer spilled his wine."

"It's not wet, must have dried." Sandy spoke as she swiftly separated the bills by denomination, keeping her eyes on the money.

Entering the small windowless room dressed in her wool suit, Caroline started to feel hot and itchy, involuntarily scratching her arms. She didn't care how much money was in those boxes, she just wanted to flee this confined space. "Paula, is there anything I can do for you?"

"If it wouldn't be a bother, we could use some new boxes and keys. It would make our jobs a lot easier. It keeps getting harder to turn these keys. They get stuck in the locks."

"I agree. Installing new keys and boxes would be a smart idea." The keys to the count room were like the keys to Fort Knox. Getting new keys would allow her to keep a tight inventory of them. "It may take some time, because I have to order them. Great job, ladies," she said, beginning to feel faint. "I'll leave you to your work." Relieved, she escaped back to the mayhem on the gaming floor.

Passing through a row of slot machines, a very angry slim woman with wiry gray hair tugged on Caroline's jacket, refusing to let her pass. "Otis Johnson would like to ban himself. He has lost most of our pension money at the slot machines. I'm his wife so I know we can't afford it."

Caroline recognized Otis, a heavy man supporting a rotund belly, playing at a video poker slot machine. A frequent guest of the casino, known for his good humor and generous tips, but tonight he seemed to have lost his sense of humor. He seemed silently mortified. His eyes pleaded for his wife to be quiet, but she wasn't paying attention.

"He has the diabetes and he needs to take care of himself. This has to stop," the woman demanded, oblivious to his embarrassment.

Despite the fact that signs were posted all over the walls advertising Gamblers Anonymous with the number *1-800-GAMBLER* prominently displayed, few people could admit to themselves that they were addicted to gambling, unaware their addiction was all too obvious to everyone around them.

Caroline turned and asked him, "Is a suspension all right with you?"

"It better be if he wants a wife to come home to," the wife sneered.

Caroline had no power to pronounce someone an addict. "The casino is very clear on this point, only a customer can ban himself."

"Ban me," a beaten down Otis said in surrender.

"Fine, you are banned from the casino for ninety days, but you can make it a lifetime ban if you would like. Go home, think about it, and let me know." She handed him her business card. "The last thing the Night Hawk wants to do is cause trouble in your marriage." She took these requests seriously because it meant Otis was in too deep. The casino didn't want to be responsible for anyone losing their home or in this case a wife.

Suddenly she wished she was back in the claustrophobic count room.

Chapter Eight

A Dealer Has to Be Able to Work on All National and Religious Holidays

Americans loved holidays, anticipated them, spent countless hours making plans on how to spend them. Since so many people preferred to spend those holidays at casinos, rather than with their families, employees of those establishments hated the holidays.

Time off was not allowed. In fact, holidays often meant working six-day weeks. As a gesture of solidarity Caroline always made sure she remained highly visible. Having no social life certainly enhanced her work ethic though sometimes she was ashamed to admit she enjoyed spending those special days with her co-workers because she needed to be around a crowd on the holidays. With no need to be alone on a holiday, there was always turkey on Thanksgiving and prime rib on Christmas to share with the other employees.

This year John stood behind a grill, cooking burgers while she dressed them for the hordes of hungry workers in the team member garden. The barbecue on Independence Day was an annual tradition.

When he had showed up earlier, holding his signature gin and tonic she had almost cried. "John, it's so great to see you! Screw political correctness, I have to hug you—it's a national holiday. This place is a madhouse. Why are you here and not lying on some beach?" She admired his dedication, he did have a life, but he always showed up.

The grill sizzled as he flipped a row of burgers. "I never forget the Night Hawk is just down the road from the Marine base. I have to let these guys know I care. So many of them have lost friends and family over there. I served in the Marines but never saw action."

She noticed the twinkle slip from his eyes. "I lost a nephew in Iraq, for what? Makes you wonder why the American government just keeps sending young men to fight for old men's greed in wars that no one ever wins. The Fourth of July is a tough day for Marines." His somber tone was highly unusual for John.

She placed her hand on his shoulder. "You taught me everyone counts. When soldiers come in and tell me this is their last night before deployment, my heart breaks." Remembering those conversations, tears welled up in her eyes.

In the months since she had come to the Night Hawk, she had grown to care for her Marine customers. Talking to them in the late hours of the night usually after a few beers, they were eager to share their stories. Just yesterday a shy private with a sweet Southern accent dripping of honey confided, "Ma'am, I'm shipping out tomorrow."

Many of the soldiers had been born after the wars started and couldn't remember a time without fighting. To them war was the natural state of the world. Her heart always broke when she realized some of them would never return home. "Come find me after your tour, and we'll fix you up with a big steak."

She always prayed she would see them again and

have to deliver on that promise. She held it together until she walked into her office, and then she put her head down on her desk and sobbed.

John smiled and waved a stack of vouchers. "I'm not going to give them some 'thank you for your service' bullshit. I come with comps." He waved a stack of vouchers. "Come help me hand these out."

For the next hour they swanned the casino searching for Marines, scanning the room for buzz cuts. They would approach them playing at slot machines or drinking at the bar. John would surprise them with a comp for fifty dollars, good for a free meal at the restaurant of their choice. The Marines always humbly thanked them.

John's phone rang just as hers began to vibrate.

She read the text message, sighed, and told him, "We have to get over to the pit. There's trouble with a capital T brewing at the high limit game."

Most people, many who have never actually entered a casino, picture a high roller as a suave James Bond type playing baccarat in a glamorous Monte Carlo setting dressed in a tuxedo. Contrasting that image, at the blackjack table they were greeted by a white guy sporting dreadlocks, his raggedy jeans falling down from his skinny frame, exposing his underwear and butt crack. She wondered when his pants would fall to the floor. His clothes reeked of marijuana, and he wore a wild gleam in his dilated eyes.

Crystal from the strip club sat beside him. To score an evening with her, he must have come loaded with cash. His eyes remained fixated on her gold glitter tube top; hers never strayed from his pile of chips. It remained a toss-up whether the casino or Crystal would get his money first. She wondered if she was working overtime for the Goldbar or freelancing.

He acted like someone who ran a meth lab in the desert, a perfect setting for cooking meth. Local television stations reported on them every week, as well as oxycontin overdoses, heroin, and the scariest drug of all, fentanyl. Tweakers were a familiar sight at the casino. Since the player wouldn't give the pit boss his name, Caroline nicknamed him Meth-head.

He stood at the table twitching all over, while at the same time spewing a manic rant, talking as he pulled wads of cash out of a brown paper bag. "Does this place employ any white dealers? Every time I play in this toilet there is always some slant eye dealing to me! I can't win with no Asian dealer, they cheat."

If she didn't work in a casino, she would have been shocked at the words coming out of his mouth. But she did work at a casino, so nothing surprised her. She tried to guess what emotions were passing through Ling's head. She doubted being abused by an asshole for being born Asian was part of her American dream.

Whatever her private thoughts, Ling's manner remained passive, her face immobile, speaking only to add up the cards. Through the years all dealers had been instructed that there were times when they needed to dummy up and deal. They were taught to follow this simple rule—when someone is giving you a hard time, don't be confrontational, just keep quiet and deal. Let management handle the problem.

Meth-head ratcheted up his ranting. He added highly erratic hand movements, waving his hands to the ceiling. He pointed at the dealer. "Look at her. She don't even smile when she steals my money. I ain't playing another hand till you get me a white dealer. I can win with a white dealer. I can't win with no chink."

John slid into the seat beside Meth-head at the table. Altercations sometimes did escalate, and this one seemed to be headed that way. He hovered around him like he was ready, even eager for action. She could sense the angry teenager in him itching for a fight.

Fed up with this idiot, Caroline said, "You will not be playing here anymore. Pick up your chips because the dealer will not deal you another hand."

She nodded to Ling and waved to the security guards approaching the table. The three security guards, poised for action, circled the player.

Caroline continued, "These young men will help you find the door."

Meth-head's wild eyes darted around the room, but then he realized he was outnumbered. Reluctantly he picked up his chips, frantically stashing them into his pockets until they overflowed onto the floor. Crystal ran around snatching up all the loose chips, stuffing them into her own pockets. When the chips had been all picked up, she disappeared—just like Meth-head's money.

He stared straight at Caroline. "I'm not done with you, bitch! I know where you work. When you aren't expecting me, I'll find you." The screaming attracted attention, and a swarm of customers surrounded the table.

John broke in. "I'm the tribal chairman. Think very carefully about what you say next. Threaten my employees again and I'll send you to jail. You are barred from this casino, forever."

With a screech, Meth-head wagged his index finger

at John, "You better watch your step too, Pocahontas."

At John's signal, security guards surrounded his seat. Meth-head was so skinny they had no trouble picking him up by his armpits and escorting him away. "I'm just joking," he yelled. "Can't any of you mother fuckers appreciate humor around here?"

The crowd cheered; a few heckled. "Pull up your pants! Wash your hair! Learn some manners!" they yelled as he was led away, accompanied by John and the guards.

Caroline watched until she saw Meth-head safely deposited outside the front door. As soon as he was gone, she leaned over the table to comfort Ling. "I am so sorry. You did a great job. I'm sorry people behave like idiots. Players are superstitious and racist, but you shouldn't have to be subjected to their prejudices." So much for creating a non-hostile work environment.

Then a great burst of spontaneous laughter erupted from Ling, the kind of laugh that only comes after times of great stress. "No problem. Sometimes I like to pretend I don't understand English."

The casino business was tough but what job wasn't? There were customers who believed they could only win with Asian dealers, or men dealers, or older dealers. Sometimes they could only win in the morning, while others believed night-time was the right time. A superstition existed for everything and an idiot ready to believe it.

Later, while depositing some dirty ashtrays at the bar, she spotted John at the other end drinking a solitary gin and tonic. He slumped over the bar, not talking to anyone.

She sat down beside him. He stared straight ahead.

"What a night. I love kicking scumbags out of here. One of the best parts of owning a casino."

His words were full of bravado, but she could see the sadness behind the eyes. He clutched his drink close to his chest. "When I was growing up in Palm Springs, the whites thought it was fun to harass us. We lived in Section Fourteen, which meant Native Americans, African Americans, and Latinos all crammed into one square mile. I will not allow anyone to treat my employees like the white kids treated us—as if we were less than them. We got casinos, and then my how things changed. Now people are checking their DNA to see if they have Shotowa blood running in them. Everyone wants to become a tribal member. They all want the money."

"Is this coming from John, the most cool, calm, and collected man I know? What is making you so maudlin tonight?"

"A smile can hide a lot. Charm becomes a tool to overcome prejudice. I know some people look at me and think I have life all figured out, but the real John has a son he rarely sees. The real John can't stick with one woman. The real John feels most at home with a gin and tonic, standing at a crowded bar talking to a stranger. Tell me the truth, is the real John a rotten person?"

"We have known each other too long for me not to be honest with you. I think you are a decent person with some human frailties, but aren't we all? We just have to learn to live with our regrets, and if you find out how, let me in on the secret. Now let's walk out to the parking lot. We don't want to miss the fireworks. You paid for them, you should be there to enjoy them."

Around midnight as she lay in her bed reading, she noticed headlights shining through her window. Peeking through the blinds, she was surprised to see a black sedan in her driveway. Who could that be, it's the middle of the night? Probably someone got lost. They will turn around in a minute she hoped. But time passed and the car remained in the driveway. Terrified, she called Brandon.

He answered on the first ring. "I'm close by, on my way home. Sit tight, don't answer the door for anyone. I'll be there in a few minutes."

Body shaking, heart pounding, she wrapped herself in the covers and waited. Time stood still until she heard Brandon's voice booming through the canyon. "Get out of the car. What are you doing here? Why are you trespassing on Ms. Popov's property? I told you to stay away from her."

Worried for Brandon, she grabbed her robe, slung it on, and ran to the porch, on unsteady legs. Shocked at the sight of Brandon holding Derrick, sprawled against his car, a gun pointed at his head. It was the first time she had witnessed violence up close.

Derrick pleaded, "I just got a job order to come here. I was hired to run a fare to the airport in Palm Springs. I swear."

"Show me," Brandon commanded.

Derrick pulled out his mobile, frantically studying the screen, and then threw it on the ground. "It's gone, the order is gone. I've been running a black cab to make some cash. I advertise on Craig's list. It was there! I swear it was there! I didn't know Ms. Popov lived here. No fucking way I would come here if I did."

"Is this your idea of a sick joke?" Caroline

screamed from the porch.

Brandon deftly swung Derrick around and punched him in the gut. "If I ever see you anywhere near Ms. Popov again, you won't be able to walk away because your legs won't work! Now you have ten seconds to get the hell out of here."

Still holding his gut, Derrick picked up his mobile phone. "This is a sick joke, but I didn't do anything. I've been fitted up. I swear."

Derrick got into his car and drove away. Frightened standing on the porch, she appealed to Brandon for guidance.

He approached the porch. "Ms. Popov, I am sure he won't be back tonight. I don't know what his intentions were, but now he knows we are onto his game. I doubt if he will bother you again, but your guess is as good as mine. Do you want me to stay here for the night? I could sleep on your couch."

Not wanting to appear weak, she reluctantly declined his offer. "Thanks, but I agree he won't be back tonight." She shivered and pulled her robe closer around her.

"You're freezing. Go back inside. You know I am close by, but as an extra precaution I will make sure the local police ride by several times."

"Thank you, so much. I don't know what would've happened if you hadn't come so quickly."

"I will always be there for you, Ms. Popov. I hope you understand that the police wouldn't have arrested him because he didn't threaten you. I also hope you know I wouldn't have shot him. But like Teddy Roosevelt said, 'Speak softly and carry a big gun.'"

She laughed. "Please call me Caroline. I mean you

might have just saved my life. I have a confession, too. Don't think I am an awful person, but I am so glad you hurt him. Derrick scares the hell out of me." She wanted to throw her arms around him but didn't want to make him uncomfortable.

He spoke her first name tentatively. "Goodnight, Caroline. I'll wait here while you go back inside and bolt the door. Promise you will call me if you get scared." He waited in the driveway until she was safely inside.

She stood at the living room window while Brandon started his engine thinking, it's a shame I can't date a co-worker.

Chapter Nine

The Graveyard Shift Is the Most Relaxed—Most of the Bosses are at Home Sleeping

Of the three shifts at the casino, the graveyard shift was the most misunderstood. Tonight, at two a.m., when most people were reaching deep REM sleep, Caroline joined a rare breed of humans who stumbled awake, careful not to disturb the others they lived with. Quietly, they dressed in the dark and sipped on coffee as they drove through the deserted streets, making their way to work. They craved the quiet of the middle of the night. The stars sparkling in the sky guided their way.

Most of the workers on the graveyard shift were there by choice, not because they drew the short straw. Some of the employees worked nights to parent their children during the day. Some enjoyed the slow pace of the work, and some just liked the shift because there were fewer bosses around which meant fewer problems for them.

When she first found herself in the casino business, she hung out on graveyard for a very long time. Her humiliation had been great, and she imagined she was hidden there. But now her job as manager required her to check up on the shift with unannounced visits.

As she stepped through the glass doors at the front of the casino, her eyes locked on the bottles and glasses strewn about. Ashtrays were overflowing. It was a tough job to keep a casino sparkling, but necessary no matter what the hour of the day. If she noticed the mess, so would customers. Nothing was less appealing than walking into a dirty casino. It was three a.m., but the late hour was no excuse for sloppiness.

Passing by a row of video poker machines, she spied Otis Johnson playing a machine in the corner. Disguised in a hat and sunglasses he tried to remain inconspicuous, but she recognized him from his wide girth. A walker parked beside his machine signaled that his diabetes had gotten worse. She was very familiar with the disease because so many of her patrons suffered from it. The more immobile they became, the more they liked to escape to the fantasy world of bells and whistles where they could forget their illness for a while. Their exercise for the day consisted of pushing buttons and pulling handles.

Immediately she called Brandon. He met her at Otis' slot machine. She patted the big man on the back. "My friend, you know you can't be here, you barred yourself from the casino. Your wife doesn't want you here, and I don't either. Your marriage is the most important thing. You probably won't believe us, but we are just looking out for you."

Embarrassed, he slowly hoisted himself up from the machine, collecting a ticket containing the balance of his credits left in the machine. Slowly pushing his walker he followed them to a cash out machine and slid his voucher into a slot on the machine where his credits turned into cash, sort of like an A.T.M. Not wanting to humiliate him, Caroline tried to make small talk as they led him to the front door.

He didn't meet her eyes, much less carry on a conversation. It wasn't the first time, and she would bet it wouldn't be the last time he would try to sneak into the casino. Only one percent of the people who gambled became addicted, but compulsive gambling was a powerful addiction, withdrawal symptoms painful, and relapses common. She escorted him out to the parking lot trying to ease his discomfort while making sure he left the casino.

An hour later, she made her way to the employee cafeteria to indulge herself with a treat for the ride home in the form of a cup of hot chocolate. While she waited for her hot chocolate to dispense from the nozzle, she noticed Paula and the count team feasting on cake and vanilla ice cream in the back corner, a single shiny balloon rising above the table.

Paula waved to her. "Come join us." She cut a piece of cake, placing it on a paper plate. She held it up for her to take. "It's my birthday and my team bought me this delicious coconut cake, my favorite, from Desert Cakes, they make the best desserts in the desert."

Fuming, Caroline refused the offer. Switching to panic mode, she demanded answers. "Who is in the count room? Has the count even been done yet? Do you have the keys?"

Paula shook her head from side to side.

Dumbfounded by the lack of attention for the rules, Caroline kept her tone just below a shout. "This is not acceptable. The count room keys are never allowed to leave the room, especially since these are new keys."

Paula didn't seem fussed at all, her round face continued beaming. "Don't worry, the keys are safe.

The count room is being guarded by security. Brandon and Hector are there holding the keys for me. The boxes have been delivered, but don't worry. They haven't been opened yet. They watch the room for us all the time."

"It doesn't matter who it is. You are the only one who is permitted to hold that key. We'll talk about this later. I have to get to the count room."

Security coupled with checks and balances kept the modern casino running. Gone were the days when the Mafia bosses opened the drop boxes and helped themselves to a cut of the winnings. She was annoyed with Brandon but would have to tread lightly when she rebuked him. She could never forget he was John's best friend.

Blood boiling, racing through the casino, she approached the count room while visions of Brandon and Hector reaching into the drop boxes, pulling out wads of cash, and stuffing it into their pockets danced through her head. After walking in to find the two of them relaxing at the table with all the boxes still locked, she breathed a sigh of relief.

She relaxed momentarily, but then remembered how pissed off she was. "You guys are my first string, you need to follow the rules, set an example. If I can't get my managers onboard with the new security measures, what chance do I have of getting the rest of the employees to follow the rules? Let me make myself clear, no one touches the key to the count room except Paula."

Brandon shrugged his shoulders. She tried to read his reaction. Being chastised by someone younger than him who wasn't even a member of the tribe, must sting.

But his face remained passive, making it hard to read his mood. "I'm sorry. We didn't mean to break the rules. I just wanted the girls to have some fun. I get it, no more parties, boss. Here, you take them." He tossed the keys to her, then saluted.

She decided to ignore his snark. "I know how important these celebrations can be for morale. I remember my first birthday as a broke and lonely dealer. I walked into the break room before my shift, feeling sorry for myself, and there on the counter sat a cake the dealers had bought me. The gesture really touched me. Don't tell anyone, but I cried."

Her mind wandered back to that day and her surprise at spying a big sheet cake, decorated in bright pink letters spelling out *Happy Birthday Caroline*, on the counter in the break room.

"Guys, I know that you have been watching the room while the girls throw their parties, but from now on they can only have cake before or after their shift. I hope you enjoy my company because I plan to join you until the count room ladies return." She picked up her cell phone. "But first I have to make a call. Paula, that cake did look delicious. Save me a piece."

And that's why she got out of bed in the middle of the night because you can't fix a problem if you don't know there is a problem.

****

"Holly, how are life and the machines treating you? Can I get you a cup of coffee?"

Management treated the bread and butter of the business, the regular customers who played at the casino a few times a week with appreciation. Amused, Caroline observed Holly Hendrix open a large floral bag with wooden handle and pull a Buddha statue from it. She placed it on the ledge of the Signs of the Universe slot machine game. The bag, full of snacks, sat open on the floor beside her. Next, she draped a Balinese shawl around her shoulders. A little pile surrounding her, she was settling in for a marathon session at her favorite machine.

"Are the stars all aligned tonight?" Caroline asked.

"Saturn has moved out of Scorpio and Jupiter has taken its place. That means this should be my lucky year. Is the casino prepared?"

Holly's wavy gray hair hung past her shoulders. Her smart phone balanced on her knees, she glanced down at the screen which displayed a chart filled with numbers and astrological signs. "Excuse me, my astrology programs show me that this is my lucky second." She pulled the lever, no matches. "Maybe next time." She laughed, an infectious laugh. "I love my slot machines."

When Caroline started in the business, electronic devices hadn't been allowed at the slot machines or the tables. No one was allowed to take a picture in the casino. But after the popularity of cell phones grew, policing their use became impossible. People would rather leave the casino than turn off their phones. The war had been lost, and now patrons posed for selfies in front of their favorite slot machines.

"Good luck. I would love for someone to win the million-dollar progressive." She rubbed Holly's hands for good luck. "Why not you?"

The casino loved it when the regulars won huge jackpots. A big payoff gave the other customers such hope. Contrary to popular opinion, a big win didn't cost the casino too much money because progressive machines were linked across many casinos.

A cocktail server passed by, carrying a tray of coffees. She grabbed one and handed the cup to Holly. "Just like you take it, black."

Another trick of the trade, all managers wrote down their customer's vital statistics and preferences in little black books. They memorized how they took their coffee and what they ordered for breakfast.

****

Money travels through casinos in mysterious ways. Caroline and John were meeting in her office to discuss the casino hold, the percentage of money the customer left on the table or in the machines.

"Check this out." She opened up a graph on her terminal. "We sped up the procedures. The dealers are getting out ten percent more hands per hour, and the hold was going up, but then in the last few months the hold on blackjack has slipped from sixteen to thirteen percent. I don't have a decent explanation why, but I am going to find one."

Most days she was grateful to have John as a boss because nothing ruffled him, but sometimes his calm demeanor exasperated her. It was hard to get him worked up about anything. His face wore an almost saintly countenance. She could tell him the table games had lost a million last night and he would remain unfazed.

"Sometimes you win, but sometimes you don't win by as much. We're still winning, aren't we?"

"I don't seem to be getting through to you. Something's not right here. I can't put my finger on it, but I will. Isn't that why you sent me here?" He promoted her to the Night Hawk to straighten up the place, but along the way he seemed to have lost interest in her mission.

"You're doing a great job. I'm over the moon with you. But I think it's past time for my gin and tonic." He did a good Dean Martin impersonation, but she believed he was sharper than that.

She followed him down to the bar because past experience taught her the bar was the best place to try and have a serious conversation with him. Rap music blasted in the background. Smoke hung like a haze over the bar. Young Marines loved the grittiness of rap, but she struggled to talk over the noise.

Suddenly, three stools away from her, a young man dressed in his civvies, but proudly wearing a Marine baseball cap, stood up and yelled at the bartender in a pronounced New York accent. "You poured them free drinks, why do I have to pay? Is it only free drinks for locals day?"

The bartender halfheartedly denied the accusations, "No bro, they paid."

Skeptical, she approached the Marine. "What seems to be the problem here?"

"I've been buying drinks at the bar all day, tipping too." He delivered his words in an aggressive drunken tone, head swaying like a bobble head doll. "Then these yokels show up and they don't pay." He pointed to a group of longhairs dressed in jeans and flannel shirts. "Please let them know Woodstock is dead!"

"Well, I can't buy you alcohol, but I can get you a cup of coffee." Caroline extended the offer, hoping to calm the situation.

"Nah, I don't feel like sobering up. I'm out of here,

but I want you to know that guy is a thief."

And that is how you catch a thief. Always believe the bystander, the person who doesn't have skin in the game. One casino guest gets mad because another guest is getting something he isn't. People love getting something for nothing but hate it when the other guy does. Surveillance didn't catch cheaters nearly as often as other customers did, therefore casino managers took seriously the accusations made by their guests. When she became a pit boss, she caught a dealer overpaying because another player at the game ratted him out. Obviously, the customer who reported him wasn't the one being overpaid.

A text appeared on her cell phone.

—*Don't let life get you down. Help is on the way. Your biggest fan.*—

She read the message then deleted it, always careful never to reply to an unknown number. She admired the creativity, even though she still couldn't figure out who was sending these texts or what they were trying to sell her.

Leaning over the screen in the surveillance room, Caroline and John searched the film of the bar. She located the exact spot in the tape and pointed her index finger at the screen. "The Marine told the truth, there's the bartender pouring free drinks for his bros. What an idiot. He will never find another job this juicy. He begged me for a promotion, then used it to steal from us. I am always such a sucker for a sob story. He said he needed to help out his parents, they were out of work. That really pisses me off."

"He probably does help them out. There aren't many decent jobs around here."

"Then tell me, if there aren't any decent jobs around, why don't they try to keep the ones they have? Did you realize that since I took over at the Night Hawk, I have been forced to fire too many employees? Each and every one of them deserved it. Some employees stole, some were no-shows at work, some were rude to customers, and some were just incompetent—they made too many mistakes. Most of them just didn't take their jobs seriously enough."

Then a revelation hit her—she had become the bystander. Since she didn't have a life, she spent her time watching other people, constantly amazed at what she discovered. For the hundredth time she told the voice in her head that she needed to get a life before she ended up a cynical piece of human wreckage.

John replied, "What can you do? You can give a man a job, but you can't stop him from stealing. He wanted to impress his bros. I know his parents. Should we give him another chance?"

"He's a nice kid who is going to learn a valuable lesson today because if he doesn't eventually, he will turn into a real thief. He has to learn. Don't bite the hand that feeds you. I was broke once, but I never considered stealing from the casino."

John interrupted her, "That is why you are on my A team, one of the people I trust."

"Then trust me now. I have learned if a person cheats once, and there are no repercussions, they will cheat again. Only next time they will just get sneakier to make sure they don't get caught. Remember, we have implemented a zero-tolerance policy on cheating. I want him gone from here today." She shook her head in frustration. A pounding building in the back of her skull. "I hate firing people, but it would do him a disservice to let him get away with stealing."

John leaned back in the swivel chair. "You can't take it so personally. It's hard to fire people you work with every day."

"I just thought it would be different. I deluded myself I could be friends with the dealers and management, even though I know everyone likes to bitch about the boss. I painted such a pretty picture in my head. Everyone would love me, no one would steal, and we would be one big happy family. The family of my imagination."

"Face facts, you can't be a double agent. You have to pick a side, and your duty is to protect the casino's assets. People don't steal to hurt you. They aren't even thinking about you, only the money. You're thinking about this situation the wrong way. Today most Night Hawk employees showed up for work, on time, and performed their jobs perfectly. Don't forget about them. Our trustworthy employees more than make up for the dishonest ones. I don't want you to get hard. I believe there's room in this casino for heart, don't you?"

She cringed in defeat. She couldn't stay mad at him for long. "How did you get to be so wise? No wonder the tribe keeps electing you chairman. I don't want to fire anyone else tonight, so I'm out of here. I'll get surveillance to write up the report, and then in the morning I will start the search for a new bartender." Sometimes it was overwhelming holding the fate of so many people in her hands.

Chapter Ten

The Shotowa Tribe Regards its Workers as Team
Members, not Employees

In olden days the Shotowa Pow Wow would have
been held on the open plains. The cloudless sky and
chocolate mountains still stood in the distance, that
hadn't changed. But today, food trucks surrounded a
giant air-conditioned tent set up in the parking lot as
protection from the intense desert sun.

The Shotowa were a powerful tribe. They owned
not one, but two casinos. The pow wow was the
highlight of a gaming conference where the leaders
from Native American nations across America gathered
at the Night Hawk. Hospitality was a hallmark of
Native culture. They showed off their status by
providing feasting, dancing, and socializing in honor of
Native culture.

Caroline took a rare Saturday off from work to
attend. Thrilled to be out of her business suit, she
arrived wearing jeans and new cowboy boots that
pinched her toes. Walking into the grand entryway, she
passed by dancers dressed in ornately beaded buckskins
and feathered headdresses waiting for their turn to
perform.

Members of the neighboring Morongo Tribe
chanted the bird dance, holding gourds in their hands

filled with palm seeds, the sound reminiscent of a baby shaking its rattle. The seats on the bleachers were filled with tribal members and locals enjoying the show. High up in the stands she spotted John chatting up a very petite dark-haired beauty. Curious, she climbed up the steps to join them.

John scooted over to make room for her. "I would like you to meet Mindy Oxendine. I like to call her my boss. She works for the Bureau of Indian Affairs. Let me introduce Caroline Popov, casino manager here."

Mindy extended a hand. "So pleased to meet you."

She immediately developed an affinity for this woman who exuded confidence and competence. Her black eyes shone and dimples appeared on the side of her mouth when she smiled, and she seemed to always be smiling. When they shook hands, it felt like they exchanged a secret handshake.

"Can you show her around?" John asked. "She'll be visiting us for a few days, checking out our operation. I have to leave now to get my son ready for his performance, help him with the headdress. It belonged to his third great grandfather who wore it when he signed the treaty with General Grant. Meet me here at two o'clock for the show." Then he slipped away. That was the thing about John, he never stuck around for long. He was hard to pin down.

Following the fragrant scent of frying grease, their noses led them to a truck offering Native cuisine. They ordered a lunch of Southwestern chili and Indian fry bread. They picked up their flimsy paper plates and set them on a picnic table.

An expression of sublime pleasure crossed over Mindy's face as she bit into the greasy confection.

"Bread deep fried in oil and dusted with powdered sugar. I really shouldn't eat this, but I can't resist because it's totally decadent and delicious."

Curious, Caroline wanted to find out as much about her as she could without seeming intrusive. "How did you end up working for the Bureau of Indian Affairs?"

"I have always been curious about my heritage. One time I caught a television show about the Lost Colony. Legend has it that the Lumbee Tribe are descendants of local tribes and the Roanoke Colony. I'm a member of the Lumbee Tribe of North Carolina. To learn more about my ancestors, I studied archeology at East Carolina. You might not have heard of the Roanoke Colony because they got lost, and once they did historians changed the name to the Lost Colony."

"The name alone sounds intriguing. Tell me more." She wiped sweat off her forehead. "This chili is spicy."

"The Lost Colony was founded in 1585 on Roanoke Island. If it had survived, it would have been the first English settlement in America. After the first year their leader, John White, sailed to England to buy supplies for the colony, but before he could return from England he got delayed by the Spanish Armada. Am I boring you?"

"Are you kidding? I love to learn new stuff. I majored in history in college. Here in California, we don't learn much about the history of the Eastern States."

Mindy grinned. "Okay then. When White returned three years later, the colony had vanished. The only clue he found in the empty village was the word 'Croatoan' carved on a tree. Croatoan was the name of an island that was home to a local tribe. What became of the settlers is one of the greatest mysteries of American history. I majored in archeology to try and find any trace of the Lost Colony."

"So did you find them?" Caroline asked.

"No, sadly they remain lost. My tribe has been fighting for federal recognition for over a century. After college I decided the best way to help was to earn a law degree and go to work at the Bureau of Indian Affairs. I am learning all I can about casinos and hopefully one day our tribe will have a casino of our own. In my job I also get to interact with so many other Native American nations. I am really proud to have a job that matters, one that helps my people."

"It really does. I see all the great things the Shotowa are doing for their members." Caroline glanced at her watch. "It's time for the dancers." Finished eating, they tossed their plates and utensils in the trash and meandered back to the performance tent.

There, they found John on the bleachers, his cousin Joanna beside him. Caroline couldn't put her finger on the reason, but Joanna always made her feel uneasy. It wasn't the words she spoke but the sharp tone she used when speaking. But maybe showing up for the pow wow would prove to Joanna that she really did have the tribe's best interest at heart.

Once the performance got underway, she immediately recognized John's son circling the dusty stage. Even dressed in rawhide wearing a feather headdress the resemblance was incredible, just as handsome as his father.

"Your son is a mini-you, destined to break hearts."

"Unfortunately, he already is. Kevin lives with his mother. Last week she found him messing about with a girl in his room when he thought she was at work. This week we are thinking about sending him to an all-male boarding school to slow him down a bit."

At that moment everyone's attention was diverted by a haunting scream emerging from one of the dancers as he jumped in the air, his feathers shaking. *"Owwwwl, owwwwl."* The teenage dancer kept howling the sound *owwwwl* at the top of his lungs, as he moved in circles over the ground.

Joanna spoke, her voice ringing with pride. "That's my son, Ahote. He is on the autism spectrum and likes to do things his own way. When he was a very young child, he heard an owl in the backyard, and became mesmerized. That was special because in our culture the owl is a symbol of ancient knowledge. He became obsessed with owls, stayed up nights tracking owls in the desert. I'm glad I named him, Ahote, which means restless one, it fits. Sometimes I think he believes he is an owl. We encourage people to express themselves. That is part of Shotowa culture."

Then an amazing thing happened. Kevin and all the other dancers begin to howl along with Ahote. The dance ended with a chorus of dancers shaking their gourds up to the sky, screaming *"Owwwwl"* over and over at the top of their lungs. Caroline was touched by the haunting sound of the singers, but more by their solidarity.

She glanced over at Joanna and saw a tear run down her cheek. She began to view the woman in a new light, raising an autistic child by herself must be so hard. Life often presented people with challenges so big they think they will never endure them, but they do, and life goes on. No wonder Joanna was so tough.

After the entertainment ended and the crowd began to disperse, she screwed up her courage and asked, "Mindy, would you like to come over to my house? We could drink wine on the porch and watch the sunset. It would be so great to have another woman to talk to."

Caroline surprised herself with her invitation. She usually wasn't this open with strangers. She tried to act nonchalant, but her heart was beating rapidly. She had a girl crush. "I'd love to. It's been a week filled with testosterone. The Pechanga, the Morongo, the Apache, the Agua Caliente, and fifty other tribes, all vying to be the big chief. I could use an estrogen fix."

That afternoon they relaxed on Caroline's porch sipping sauvignon blanc, watching the sky explode in streaks of orange and red. Encouraged by the alcohol, she shared with Mindy the tale of how she came to live alone in a cabin in the desert.

Chapter Eleven

Palm Springs, California, October 2009

The dull throb of a small hangover played in the back of John Tovar's mind, like a small hammer tapping him on the head. Coughing from a scratchy throat, he stopped by the gift shop to buy his morning can of cola. The caffeine helped. For relief he held the chilled can against his forehead. He hated to admit to himself that he was a functioning alcoholic, in part because it fit the stereotype of the drunken Indian, but he convinced himself that he functioned really well. Soda in hand, he walked to the hotel desk to pick up the daily comp report.

The report told him which players were using their points at the casino hotel. John liked to review it to keep track of who was staying on property. He aimed to touch base with his red card holders during their stay. He hoped this personal touch set his properties apart from the other casinos in the area. From what he observed, most tribal chairmen only stepped into their casinos to pick up their checks. Scanning the list, a familiar name caught his eye. Caroline Popov.

For the last few months she had been absent from the Palm Oasis, most likely because she split with her husband Andrei. Rumors spread, they had given up gambling. He worried about them because when people stopped playing, it usually wasn't because they had won too much money.

His tribe had only been in the casino business for ten years, but his emotions were conflicted. He loved that for the first time the tribe was self-sufficient, but he didn't like seeing people throw their life savings away on silly games. Growing up Shotowa, survival had been a daily struggle for his single mother, while so many of the city's inhabitants lived lives of luxury hidden behind the high walls of their grand estates. Unlike some other tribal members, he never developed a taste for gambling. He played a few times at other tribal casinos just to support the other tribes, but losing money just wasn't his thing.

In an ideal world people would only wager what they could afford to lose, but in the real world people loved the thrill of gambling. Not all of them but the vast majority of their customers kept their gambling under control because very affluent people lived in Palm Springs, people who could afford the occasional night out at the casino.

He had assumed that Andrei and Caroline could afford their trips to the casino. He believed the couple embodied true love, something that always eluded him. The pair genuinely seemed to enjoy each other's company. In the past whenever he glanced their way in the restaurant they were always chatting. He found them refreshing. So many other couples ate their dinner in stony silence. He spoiled them a little bit. Andrei projected so much confidence, and she appeared to be his rock. She rarely played blackjack herself but often stood behind him rubbing his shoulders. He hoped losing at the casino hadn't played a part in their split.

He dialed her hotel room. After a few rings she picked up. "Hi, this is John Tovar. I wanted to check in with you. We've missed you at the casino. I want to hear all about your cruise to Russia. Better yet meet me over dinner, and you can tell me all about your trip."

She paused before speaking, and he could hear the sadness in her voice. "Andrei isn't with me. He stayed in Russia for personal reasons."

"Okay, then I'll make reservations for just the two of us. Meet me at the Steak House at seven. I won't take no for an answer. Tell the hostess you're with me." He was careful not to let it slip that he already learned about the split and hung up quickly not giving her a chance to protest.

Chapter Twelve

The Best Real Estate Agents Work in Teams

Caroline hung up the hotel phone, wondering how she would get through this dinner. When he called, John had probably expected to have dinner with an entertaining Andrei, and now he found himself stuck with her, the consolation prize. From the first time she met Andrei he had brought color to her ordinary life. Now that he was gone all the color had disappeared. Broke, aimless, and excruciatingly lonely, beige again. If she had a do over, would she pass on that brokers' open house that day?

Had she ever been that young? A recent college graduate working with her best friend in real estate, because she didn't have any idea of what she wanted to do? She remembered opening her empty appointment book, a flyer slipped out on the seat, advertising a brokers' open house in Naples, a charming waterfront community located right beside Long Beach. She rationalized, well, at least I'll get to eat. Brokers' open houses were a perk of the real estate business, a place where struggling newbies could cop a free lunch.

Opening the front door she was greeted by a very tall and insistent man. "Please can you help me? I need someone to pass out these sandwiches." Without waiting for an answer, he handed her a pair of tongs and pointed to a granite counter loaded with cupcakes and croissant sandwiches. "Please, you will save my life."

He sounded frantic, but in her short career in real estate, she noticed that most agents acted like drama queens. She liked his direct manner and the trace of a foreign accent she couldn't quite place. When a gondola passed by on the canal in back of the house, a perfect way to showcase the view, she wondered if the tall man had arranged such a perfect detail.

To Caroline the tall man resembled Zane, a character from her favorite soap opera. She found the sexual tension between the headstrong Kylie and the traditional Zane mesmerizing, a love affair for the new millennium. Being here, part of a cozy domestic scene, she began fantasizing that this tall dark mysterious stranger really was Zane in disguise. She pretended the two of them were hosting their first party at their new waterfront home.

After the last broker walked out the front door, the tall man approached her. "Thank you, can you believe the turnout? I should be selling this place in a week even though it looks like a prison!"

He leaned against the stainless-steel staircase bisecting the living room. "My name is Andrei Popov and you are?"

She grinned, pleased that he shared her sense of taste. "I am Caroline Fleming. You're correct. This place does look like a prison—if prisons came with water views."

"Caroline Fleming, I am famished, and I know you didn't get a chance to eat. I say we clean up this mess and you will allow me to buy you dinner. Before you protest, you saved my life so you cannot refuse me."

He repeated her name. Personalization was one of the first things she learned in real estate sales class. If you want to remember someone's name, you say it out loud because everyone loves the sound of their own name. They smiled shyly at each other. She gazed up into his big brown eyes, which had the longest lashes she had ever seen on a man. When you were six feet tall, looking up was a marvelous thing. "I will go to dinner with you if you promise to tell me how you managed to snag this listing."

She wasn't gullible or naïve. Okay, maybe a little gullible, but she would be going home by herself tonight. She realized certain people thought of her as guarded, but it paid to be careful in a scary world filled with date rape drugs and STD's. Still a virgin at twenty-three, not for religious or personal reasons, but because there was nothing casual about her, including sex.

She wanted her first time to be special, and from what she had observed, lots of her friends hooked up, but most of them didn't seem very satisfied with the results. What college guys wanted was a drunken wham-bam-thank-you-ma'am. Most didn't want relationships. Casual hook ups didn't interest her in the least. Her memories of awkward attempts at seduction using practiced lines made her laugh. Besides there was plenty of time to hold out for the real thing. She wanted Zane. She wanted forever.

After dinner he insisted on escorting her to her car. He leaned in, instead of the full-on kiss she expected, he planted a gentle peck on her forehead. She drove away, wistfully, aware that he left her wanting more.

Their romance progressed quickly, within three months a nervous Caroline sat at a booth facing the water, tapping her fingers on her knees, waiting for her best friend. She met Erica Evergreen in college. They both played basketball. She chose their favorite restaurant, the Rusty Whale, a beautiful bayside seafood house located in Newport Harbor. Newport was a rich town and people here loved to indulge in their wealth. From her seat on the glassed-in patio, she gazed down on luxurious yachts traveling up and down the harbor.

For weeks, tension had been brewing between Erica and Andrei, but wasn't there always tension between best friend and boyfriend? Everyone said they looked like sisters, but she believed that Erica, a statuesque brunette was the pretty one, even though she talked like a Valley girl. The first time Andrei met her, Caroline carefully studied his reaction to her. There had been none. He preferred her. For once she didn't feel like second choice.

Caroline laid down her fork, took a deep breath, and decided she couldn't procrastinate anymore. "You know I have been dating Andrei for a while. Since we are planning for our future, we have decided I will go work with him. We are going to be a team."

Erica always the skeptic replied, "Married, come on, like, you barely know him. Our agency, like, has a pretty affluent customer base. Be realistic, he just wants access to our customers. He's using you, and, like, pretty soon he will have gotten what he wants, and then, like, what are you going to do? You'll be dumped without a job, you'll lose everything, all for some loud, obnoxious, pushy Russian."

True to form she belittled the one thing Caroline cherished: Andrei's love.

Overcome with rage, Caroline escalated the fight, uttering the words no single woman ever wants to hear. "You're just jealous because you don't have anyone." As soon as those words escaped her lips, she shuddered.

She wasn't naïve, Erica had recently appeared on a new dating show where an eligible bachelor chose between twenty-five women. She was still stinging at having been dumped the week before the bachelor picked the final four and traveled to their hometowns to meet their families. Caroline never realized that she possessed the capacity to be so cruel and was surprised by how much she enjoyed fighting back.

No papers needed to be filed to end a friendship, but lack of paperwork didn't mean their separation hadn't been bitter and final. Caroline hadn't seen Erica since she stormed away from the table. Now she regretted her harsh words. She wondered if her ex-friend was happy.

That night Caroline left the restaurant exhilarated. Now she would start to cast her own shadow, step into the limelight, and become the star of her own story, all because of Andrei.

She finished her dinner, drove home, packed up her belongings and carried them to Andrei's apartment. A feeling of sexual power coursed through her body as she pulled her best satin nightgown over her head. She decided to replace the bad memories of the evening with positive ones, determined that after tonight she would no longer be a virgin, confident in her decision. Andrei hadn't been appalled by her virginity, he was touched by her virtue. He remained respectful of her. Sure, they fooled around a bit, but he never tried to close the deal.

She led him to his bed and whispered into his ear, "Tonight's the night!"

"Are you sure? We've waited so long." He seemed eager and apprehensive at the same time. "I just want to make sure you won't regret this."

"I have never been so sure of anything." She grabbed his hand and placed it on the band of her panties. "I'm ready."

Trembling, he took his time exploring her waiting body. His lovemaking was gentle.

Ecstatic when he penetrated her, she moaned. "Always only you."

The night he proposed was also the night they bought their first property. Andrei stopped the car in front of a small wooden duplex, situated on a postage stamp lawn. "Yesterday I put an offer on this property, it seemed like the deal of a lifetime, but today it just looks shabby." Peeling siding hung off the walls, loose shingles curved on the roof, and cracks laced the concrete driveway. "I hope you can visualize the future I see. I know that this place doesn't look great now. But we can make it beautiful. This part of Long Beach is on the rise, and we can be a part of it. You see, we stay in one apartment while we fix up the other side to rent it out." He entwined his hand with hers. "If we work hard, we can get rich. In America we make the life, life doesn't make us. We are home."

A Monarch butterfly landed on a bird of paradise planted in the yard. "Don't you see, Andrei, that's a sign? Let's do this."

****

Their Las Vegas wedding had been perfect, just the two of them. The limousine pulled up to their pyramid shaped hotel at eight p.m. sharp. The chauffeur held the door open for Andrei and Caroline as they climbed into the back. Sliding into the plush seat she tried to calm her racing heart. The marriage license bureau stayed open twenty-four hours a day—in case anyone got the urge to tie the knot in the middle of the night. He twisted the cork off the bottle of champagne included in their wedding package. The cork popped and bounced off the ceiling. The Vegas Strip was jammed with pedestrians, they sipped bubbly champagne while they enjoyed the show outside the window. The slow traffic rewarded them with plenty of time to take in the view on their trip to City Hall. Billions of lights illuminated the night sky. Fountains danced for them. At a red light they watched a volcano erupt spewing red-hot lava into the sky. Andrei squeezed her hand and she squeezed back. The feel of his big hands holding hers calmed any last apprehensions running around in her head.

After they left City Hall, marriage license in hand, a tipsy Caroline serenaded Andrei on the short drive to the chapel. "Take me to the chapel, because I want to marry my Russian Knight and live happily ever after." They pulled up to a small white building surrounded by a white picket fence, located right on the Strip, the perfect place to exchange vows. Their chaplain, a stylish woman, performed their vows.

Hands shaking, Caroline carried a bouquet of red roses and Andrei tucked a white carnation boutonniere in his jacket pocket, all part of their superior package she had purchased over the Internet.

She walked down the aisle while a Marc Cohn song about true companions played in the background. The song her special request. Everyone was searching for a true companion. Grateful, she had found hers. She joined Andrei at the altar.

He whispered, "You are so gorgeous." No one had ever cherished her the way he did. Her heart pounding, her feet unattached from her legs, wobbly, she prayed the panic attack would stop. Tears began streaming down her face.

She wondered what Andrei's family in St. Petersburg thought witnessing her meltdown at her own wedding, as they watched on their home computer. They probably worried he was marrying a lunatic. Miraculously she made it through the ceremony, although she couldn't remember a single vow she recited. She was glad they pre-bought the video. Finally, the last vows had been exchanged and hasty kisses delivered. Leaving the chapel, officially a wife, she glanced down at her finger, a real solid platinum band circled it. Although she couldn't tell you how it got there.

Life proceeded on schedule for the newlyweds. She had often been warned the first year of marriage was the hardest, but for her it had been the easiest year of her life. The latest research showed that being in love produced the same effect as taking oxycontin, it triggered serotonin production in your brain. She believed it because she had become addicted, her husband was her drug. Every time she glanced across the real estate office and watched him chatting with a customer, a chill ran through her body. Andrei was her hit, her fix, like a romance novel come to life.

They spent the first year of marriage working real estate by day and fixing up their duplex at night, hoping to rent it for top dollar. To celebrate their anniversary they decided to spend the weekend exploring Palm Springs. Andrei loved celebrations. They celebrated every time they sold a house, and birthdays were huge. He would come home with flowers, chocolates, and lots of presents. Always the one for grand gestures, the kind that sweep you off your feet, and at six feet three he's about the only person who could do it.

In real estate, the hunt was always on for the next best place. Andrei decided that Orange County had been played out, was too expensive.

Their excitement grew as the iconic Palm Springs sign began to appear in the distance, the name of the city written in a large cursive script announcing their arrival, slowly came into focus. "I can't believe I have never been here. It is gorgeous, mountains covered with flowers. I never expected to see so many flowers in the desert," a surprised Caroline gushed. An explosion of purple and gold lantana ran up and down the hillsides.

Andrei stopped the car by the side of the road so they could admire the view. "I am in awe. This place is truly unlike any other city in a desert, and I can tell you why there are so many flowers. I read about this. There are hundreds of underground springs." Andrei beamed. "I have studied all about Palm Springs. Ask me a question."

"How do they get to open a casino downtown? Aren't California casinos usually on reservations? By the way, why do Native Americans get to operate casinos?"

"You asked three questions but luckily I know the answers to all of them. Palm Springs is a reservation, well at least half of it is. The city was established in 1876 by Ulysses S. Grant, the man who won the Civil

War. Native Americans get to open casinos because each tribe is considered a sovereign nation. In 1987 the Supreme Court ruled that a state could not prohibit gambling on a reservation if the state allowed gambling. The Shotowa Tribe owns half of the city. Decades before the casinos opened, Palm Springs became popular because of the hot springs running beneath the city."

Andrei had booked a room at the Palm Oasis, a hotel with a casino located in the heart of downtown. They made reservations to have dinner in the Steak House. The waiter led them to a wrought iron table situated on an outside patio. In the distance the San Jacinto Mountains loomed over them. The sky streaked with stars, the signature night sky of the desert. "Andrei, this is so beautiful and quiet. There is no traffic on the streets. It really is a little piece of paradise."

"This real estate market is incredible. Houses here are twice the size and half the price of Orange County. We can sell the duplex and put money down on five houses here. Can you imagine five houses?" He paused to let the number sink in. "It is a gamble, but if you don't gamble you can't win. Real estate is like the stock market, you always have to be searching for the next big thing."

He was signing the check, and they were enjoying their last sips of wine when a very handsome man, his long hair plaited into a braid, stopped at their table. "Hello, I am John Tovar, Shotowa tribal chairman. I noticed the two of you sitting there and I have rarely seen a couple look so happy. What is your secret? I just wanted to come over and introduce myself. And you are?" She noticed the slow soft cadence of his speech, it gave meaning to every word.

"We are Andrei and Caroline Popov, real estate agents in Newport." Andrei stood up, shook John's hand, and retrieved one of his business cards from his wallet. He extended his card to John. Andrei never missed a chance to give someone his card. He taught her the value of little gestures. His motto was a card costs a dime but the return could be thousands. He passed them out to everyone he met.

In return John handed them his own card printed on heavy paper with his name embossed in gold print. "If there is anything I can do to make your visit more enjoyable, please let me know. Are you celebrating anything special this weekend?"

"It is our one-year anniversary, so we are staying in the hotel," Caroline blurted out. She wanted to share her happiness with everyone.

"Let me help make your anniversary even more special. I will tell the hotel to upgrade you to the honeymoon suite. I have never had much success with wedded bliss, though I keep trying. Perhaps you two can be my inspiration. Just stop by the front desk after your meal. Let me make all the arrangements."

After John left, Andrei and Caroline grinned. Radiating happiness, they high fived each other across the table. "I know John was just flattering us, but I don't care. Score! He gave us the honeymoon suite. Let's change rooms, but afterwards let's hit the tables. I believe the Popovs are on a winning streak."

Shivering she wrapped her sweater around her as the night air chilled the desert.

****

Strolling along the main drag the next day, they passed by restaurants where misters cooled the hot desert air. Caroline pointed to the sidewalk. "Andrei, look down, they have stars on the pavement just like in Hollywood. There's John's. He must be a big deal. It reads, *beloved Tribal Chairman of the Shotowa Tribe*. I knew he was special, but this is extra special." The weekend convinced them they needed to live in Palm Springs. Within a few months they had made the move and their fate had been sealed.

Once they settled in, they became regulars at the casino. It was just a few blocks from the real estate office where they worked. They indulged in the desert heat as they walked. Palm Springs resisted chain stores. Mom and pop stores lined the streets. Being located in the middle of a thriving downtown, instead of a bypass on the freeway like the other casinos, gave the Palm Oasis a more sophisticated vibe than other California casinos. It resembled a mini-Vegas. When Andrei opened the doors to the restaurant, they were blasted by air-conditioning. They ordered their usual at the Steak House, rib eyes and baked potatoes. The soothing sounds of Frank Sinatra piped into the dining room set the mood.

The waiter delivered a bottle of Beaujolais Villages nouveau. "Chairman Tovar wants you to have this," he said with a nod for John who waved at them from a spot across the room.

The night was always a little bit more special when he was in attendance, commanding the room while perched on a high stool at the bar eating his dinner, taking time out to chat with the bartender and the customers who passed him on their way to their tables.

He shook hands with the men and hugged the ladies. Not only was he the tribal chairman, the couple grew to believe he was the heart and soul of the casino. These personal touches seduced them, made them feel at home at the Palm Oasis.

Later, broke but content, they drove home to their condo in the Las Palmas district—no fancy house for them. They bought a simple condo and rented out their houses. The place was a steal on a street most people didn't even know existed, a real mid-century actually built in the middle of the century.

It might be just a condo, but it was on the same street where Kirk Douglas and many Hollywood celebrities lived. The complex that had been built in the sixties for the mistresses of the studio executives making it possible for them to live in close proximity to the mansions the studio executives shared with their wives. Being in such close proximity they could sneak out for some afternoon delight. Glass sliding doors opened to a large lanai, an outdoor living room facing out toward chocolate brown mountains. Sleepy, they leaned against the banister and gazed down at an Olympic size swimming pool, an orange flame flickering in the fire pit. The rooftops of those huge mansions loomed in the distance.

Andrei said, "I feel like we are fortunate people living in a magical place. The desert loves us. I have found my American dream."

They stood on the patio, arms entwined. It was in these quiet moments Caroline realized how truly blessed they were. It was wonderful to be married to a happy man. "I feel it too, we belong here. The desert didn't put a spell on me, you did."

Taking her hand he led her to the padded lounge chair on the patio. "Let's break this in."

He lay down on top of her. A warm breeze bathed their bodies as they slipped out of their clothes. The sweet, spicy scent of the palm blossoms hanging from the tall trees swaying in the distance filled the air. All the forces of nature combined to provide the backdrop for another perfect night in paradise. They made love by the light of the fire pit until the sun peeked from behind the mountains.

****

And then came *The Great Recession*, when everything fell apart. Since real estate was slow, they took a rare vacation, a cruise to the Baltic and a long delayed visit to Andrei's parents. After dinner with all the relatives, they went for a walk, so he could share his childhood haunts.

The scene by the Neva River completely transformed itself at night, turning into a lover's lane. They joined other couples strolling hand in hand beside the muddy river. The benches were filled with young lovers taking advantage of a long summer night. Spotting an empty bench Andrei grabbed her hand and led her over to it.

Once they were seated, he pivoted his attention to her, his face filled with exhilaration mixed with anxiety. "Ca, do you really love it here? I worried you would hate Russia."

"I love it because this is where you are from. This place made you the incredible man you are."

"This is an excellent thing. I do not know how to tell you. I have been searching for the words for weeks. We will be staying here." He spoke the words as if everything was settled.

She asked, genuinely puzzled, "Has the cruise been extended? I don't understand."

"I can't go back to America. I hope and pray, you will stay with me."

Astonished that she had traveled to Russia only to be greeted by an unsettling reality. "Andrei you are joking, right?"

"Ca, we're broke. Our houses are about to be foreclosed on. We have to stay in Russia. Here we will find a way out of this fucking mess I have created."

His face looked different and, for a man who never cursed, he dropped the F-bomb. Could it be true? Was he serious? She gazed into his eyes. Even though she didn't want to believe the perfect life they created was over, when she read the look of defeat written all over his face, she had to.

"I don't care about the houses. The bank can take them. We don't need much. We can start over." Shocked, she grabbed his arm and began crying and pleading. "We are in this marriage for the long haul. Remember history is on our side. Real estate will recover, it always does." She used words from his sales pitch, whatever platitudes she could think of to encourage him to change his mind.

He began to weep inconsolably. "We owe the bank two million dollars. I loved the casino. You win, you lose, but most of the time the losing is more than the winnings. Then one day you realize how deep a hole you have dug, a hole so big you wish you could just throw yourself in it. In America I believed the money would flow forever, like the Neva." He picked up a stone and threw it in the river.

"We will lose everything and then owe a huge tax bill. If we stay in the U.S., we will be broke until we are dead. It isn't just us. I convinced so many people to buy houses. How can I face those people? Our customers. They put their trust in me. I have let everyone down."

Fat tears were streaming down both of their faces, but they were in Russia, so no one even noticed because Russia is filled with sadness. She retrieved a tissue from her purse and dabbed the tears from his eyes.

The hour was late; the sun had set by the time they finished talking. Envious of the young innocent couples passing by them on the path. She wished they could wind the clock back to an uncomplicated time. Could she do it? Could she give up her country?

Then she remembered a technicality that might end this nightmare. "We can't leave the ship. We don't have passports." The cruise line wouldn't let anyone take their passport off the ship, for fear that they would be lost or stolen.

He reached into the inside pocket of his sports jacket and retrieved two passports. "I told them we needed them for some legal matters. I also put some clothes in with the presents. We will get the ship to send us the rest of our clothes later."

All of his secrecy crushed Caroline. "You planned all of this without consulting me?"

"I know it was wrong, but every time I tried, I couldn't find the words to explain the mess I have made. The day I met you I promised to take care of you, and I ruined everything. It was smooth on paper but... I forgot about the ravines, Old Russian proverb. But I promise I will make things right. I know I can still do it, only now I will do it here. Russia is starting over, and so will we. It will be better because I am home."

"But it is not my home," Caroline reminded him.

He put his thumb under her chin and raised her face to his. "Ca, I promise you it will be." She melted when he called her Ca, his special nickname for her.

They returned to the apartment and broke the news to Andrei's parents, glossing over the enormous amount of debt they were in. His parents were confused but delighted to have their son back. Exhausted, they fell into bed in Andrei's old room. A few hours later in the darkest part of the night, Caroline woke with a start, and all at once it hit her in the gut. She couldn't stay. Quiet as a mouse, she dressed quickly, then tiptoed over to Andrei's jacket hanging from a chair and retrieved her passport. She slipped out the front door and walked down the street toward the river searching for a taxi.

After several blocks a taxi finally approached, she handed the driver a postcard with a picture of the ship on the front. Since few of the passengers could read Cyrillic, the Russian language, the ship had given each passenger a postcard so they could hand it to the taxi drivers, who could read the name of the ship. Picture in hand the drivers could see where the cruise ships docked. The Regal Princess was not sailing until four a.m. to allow for the return of the Moscow excursion. Most of the passengers flew to Moscow, toured the Kremlin, and ended the night with a performance of the Bolshoi ballet.

Upon arriving at the ship's terminal, Caroline climbed out of the taxi and up to the Italian officer standing guard at the gangway. "How long till the ship sails?"

"The ship will be leaving as soon as the bus from

Moscow arrives. Are you coming aboard, Miss?"

"In a minute, I need some fresh air." Searching for a way to delay her boarding if only for a few more minutes. Once she boarded, they would not let her off. She didn't know if she could really leave Andrei. Staying here would be easy for him, he was Russian. His problems would be solved if he remained in Russia. If she stayed here, her problems would multiply.

Pacing up and down the dock, while the bus from Moscow arrived and the tired passengers wearily trudged up the gangway, she realized whether she decided to leave or stay, her decision would be life changing. Then she remembered her life was already screwed. Her only choice was to return to California and fix everything. *Why did Andrei do this to us?*

She remembered the Russian proverb he shared on their wedding day. The woman is the neck and the man is the head, and the head follows the neck. Caroline reasoned, *I am the neck. He will follow me home.*

The ship's horn gave two long blasts, letting everyone know that the ship would soon be leaving the dock. Her heart began to pound, and she felt the now familiar feeling of losing sensation in her legs. Reluctantly she approached the gangway, took out her cruise card, and passed it to security. Knowing that she was facing the moment of no return, she stumbled across the gangway.

Upon arriving onboard, she informed the purser Andrei would not be returning due to personal family problems. With a heavy heart she opened the door to their cabin where his clothes still hung in the closet. She put on one of his T-shirts and climbed into the bed cradling his pillow in her hands. Holding it up to her nose breathing in the familiar scent of Andrei. She alternated between crying and cursing until she ran out of tears. Their lives were so entwined, she didn't know how she would survive without him. As the sun rose, she fell asleep and didn't notice the ship sailing out of the bay and into the Baltic Sea. She woke up a few hours later, terrified of a life without Andrei.

She could never explain this to John, the casino had given them the cruise. John spoiled them. She imagined it was because like her, he was taken with Andrei. There were no words to convey how she betrayed the only man she ever loved.

Chapter Thirteen

The Casino Business Is Not for Sissies

John's mood sank as he observed Caroline entering the restaurant. She seemed bewildered and the light had vanished from her eyes. Maybe she wasn't quite beautiful, her face a little too broad and her lips too thin, but she inhabited her space with a quiet elegance. Her wavy hair hung limp around her shoulders. Tonight she wore jeans and a T-shirt instead of the immaculate suits he was used to seeing her in. The last wife had been a fancy dresser. She taught him how to tell a designer outfit from a copy, a ploy to make sure he would only buy her the real thing.

He fumbled for words after he ordered his usual gin and tonic and a bottle of sauvignon blanc for Caroline. He didn't have a clue what they would talk about. Maybe that was the problem with his marriages, he never got the hang of sharing. Serious conversations made him want to run, and he usually ran all the way out the other end of the marriage. "I hope all is well with Andrei's family?"

"They're fine. More than fine, actually, they are lovely." A wistful sigh left her chest. "It's Andrei and I, we are having problems," she spoke directly, no pretense with this girl. She was trying to hold it together, appear stoic. "We're broke, everything is gone. I am using the last of our comp points to stay in the hotel." He could see the tears dripping down her cheek. These days in the aftermath of the economic collapse it seemed like everyone cried all the time.

He handed her his napkin to dry her eyes. "It wasn't gambling, was it?" He didn't know what he would do if her answer was yes. No casino ever issued a refund. That wouldn't set a good precedent.

"Of course it was gambling, but not the kind you think. We gambled our future on real estate, only we didn't know we were gambling. But if you really want to know, playing here didn't help either."

John breathed a sigh of relief, they didn't go broke because of the casino. The fallout of the real estate collapse was on display everywhere. A record number of houses were being foreclosed. Building at many new subdivisions in the area had been abandoned mid-construction. "Quite a few of the dealers have lost their properties. But didn't you have vacation rentals, and weren't they always booked?"

"Andrei tried to explain the details to me, but I never paid much attention. Finances were his department. The original loans were no docs, written for three years, interest only. The payments were quite low. We thought it would be easy to refinance to a fixed rate loan after a few years because the properties would have gone up in value. Real estate always goes up, right? Joke's on me."

John had lived long enough to know how often real estate fluctuated. When he was younger, he witnessed the Savings and Loan Scandal of the 1980s, but now wasn't the time to bring up ancient history. So he just nodded his head, indicating that he wanted her to continue her story.

"Real estate values have plummeted, so I can't refinance anything. No bank will write us new loans. They don't care how much rental income we generate. The story gets worse. Andrei fell behind on our taxes. He didn't always pay the quarterly taxes. Also, Andrei and I were gambling our income away. I don't blame him, I enjoyed being here as much as he did. So now I am staying in the hotel using the last of our comp points until I figure out where to live next. Thanks for listening. I don't have anyone to talk to. One day you think you have it all, and the next day you find out it was a mirage. As you get closer, the future you see in the distance just disappears."

"Please, feel free to stay in the hotel room for as long as you need to. I feel like it is the least I can do." An idea was forming in his head. He decided to go with his instincts. "Come to work for me."

"You don't have to give me a job out of pity."

"I would never give anyone a job out of pity. I need you more than you need me. This is a young industry; it needs smart people. Believe me, it's hard to find reliable, honest people out here in the desert."

"You would hire a gambler for your casino?"

"I have a hunch if you go to work in my casino, you'll never want to gamble again. The tribe will send you to dealing school, start you out in the slot department until you pass your dealer training." He raised a hand, signaling he wasn't finished. "Be under no illusions, the job won't be easy. This is a tough business. Let's see if you've got what it takes." He grinned. "You know, when I needed a fresh start, the tribe lent me a helping hand. After ten years in the

Marines, I didn't know what kind of job I could get as a civilian."

"You were made for this job," she insisted.

"It might seem like that now. Indio Springs opened a bingo hall, and since I was Native American, they hired me. After a few weeks, I learned running a bingo hall was like a printing press for making money. I decided gambling was the future for the Shotowa. Inspired, I went to my tribal council and told them if they paid for my college, I would get a business degree, and find a way that we could open a casino." He waved his arms around the room. "Mission accomplished."

"Now about you. I know you have a degree, that's a plus. You are tall, which must account for something. You already have a work wardrobe. Don't throw those suits away because one day you will be promoted to manager and having a wardrobe already will save you some money." He figured if he acted like her employment was a done deal it would be.

"I love a challenge and I do need a job. But I will have to declare bankruptcy and settle up with the IRS. Surely my money problems have to disqualify me, my credit is ruined." She genuinely seemed worried.

"I promise I will make sure you get a gaming license. It's okay to declare bankruptcy, you just can't lie about anything. Put everything on your application. If you tell the truth, I promise you will be fine. Unless you can think of any other objections the matter is settled. Don't doubt me, I am an excellent judge of character, not wives. Or maybe my ex-wives were an excellent judge of my character."

The flicker of a smile crossed her face. "But do you need me? In this tough economy business must be bad."

Leaning closer, he said confidentially, "Let me let you in on a little secret. When times are good, people gamble. When times are bad, people gamble more."

The slightest nod of his head brought a waiter from across the room to take their order. The aroma of steaks sizzling filled the restaurant.

Her eyes began to crinkle, then her lips began to turn up at the corners, and a smile spread until it filled her entire face. "Something smells great. I think I'll have a rib eye. You know for the first time in weeks I feel hungry." When a gorgeous hunk of well marbled prime meat arrived at the table, she picked up her knife and fork and didn't put them down until every last bite was devoured.

John left the restaurant happy. Even though he couldn't give her back her money, he could offer her a fresh start, a new career. Teach a man to fish, teach a woman to deal, same thing. He recognized something special about her, and it wasn't romance. She clearly still loved Andrei, and he wouldn't take advantage of her vulnerable state. Instead, this could be the start of a beautiful friendship.

Chapter Fourteen

A Dealer Must Be Able to Concentrate, Ignoring All the Distractions Around Her

The first time Caroline stepped behind a table resembled an out-of-body experience. She'd recently passed her six-week course at the in-house dealing school. Today she'd be shadowed by a real dealer. No casino that wanted to stay in business would send a break-in on the floor without an experienced shadow. Abigail, a pretty redhead, stood behind Caroline, making sure she followed all the procedures and most importantly verifying that her payouts were correct. With someone observing her, and a table full of eyes attached to the bodies of seven players staring up at her, she began to feel the pressure, like an actress working on stage, standing under hot lights. A live game was much more intense than the games in dealing school, the true definition of multi-tasking.

On the floor, she needed to concentrate, blank out the band playing in the lounge, ignore the noise of the slot machines, pay no attention to the people milling around in front of her, remember to clear her hands, and keep her eyes peeled on the table, all while maintaining the disposition of a saint.

Before moving to table games, she'd worked a stint in the slots department. Slot players were an easy solitary bunch, content to escape the world by pushing a button and fixating on computer generated mermaids, wizards, kitty cats, or a thousand other images carefully designed to keep their eyes on the screen. Her job consisted of wandering the casino floor, making change for the players, and paying out jackpots. Slot players were much like those who favored the lottery. Both prayed for the big win, and they played at the casino because it ran a lottery every night. By this point, she'd worked in the business long enough to know that table games players were a different, more social breed.

She stood behind and tapped the shoulder of the dealer at her first table. The outgoing dealer stepped to the right and exited. As Caroline stepped into place, the haze of cigarette smoke drifted up her nose. The shrill voice of a highly inebriated young woman greeted her. "Are you going to be nice to us?"

Abigail whispered in her ear, "You're going to hear annoying things about a thousand times tonight. Don't forget to burn a card, and don't forget to clear your hands when you walk up to the table."

The dealers slapped their hands together and presented their palms up to the cameras: when they pushed into a table, when they cashed in money to ensure they didn't palm any of the bills, before they dropped a tip to make sure they weren't adding extra chips, and when they left the table to make sure they were leaving empty handed. She probably "cleared her hands" a thousand times that night but was sure she'd forgotten a thousand other times.

"Of course I am," Caroline answered, while concentrating on a hundred little details, a nervous smile plastered on her face. She discarded the first card out of the shoe, placing it in the discard rack, then began to deal out the hands.

"How you running?" Inebriate's boyfriend demanded. "Are you hot or cold?"

Abigail whispered again, "Ignore him."

This became Caroline's introduction to "dummy up and deal". Most questions were rhetorical and couldn't be answered or if they were answered truthfully, the players wouldn't like the answers.

She dealt two cards face-up to each player before dealing the last card to herself, that card was an ace.

"Insurance, insurance," she asked while waving her hand across the insurance line stenciled on the green felt of the table. No one bought insurance, a sucker's bet. She slid her cards into the sensor. The sensor lit up, signifying a ten-value card underneath.

"Blackjack," she announced, followed by the groans of a disappointed table. While the players complained, she turned her cards over and picked up all their money. Just her luck, the first live hand she dealt was blackjack.

Throughout the long night, overlapping customer comments varied in degree of inanity, tone of voice, and frequency, pummeling her from all sides.

"You're cheating, aren't you? You don't want me to win, do you?"

"When's your break? Pit boss, she can go on break now."

"I don't like you. You don't smile when you take my money."

"I don't like her. Look how she smiles when she takes my money."

It was as if the customers completely ignored the

fact she worked for tips. Didn't they know that all dealers in the casino wanted them to win?

Sometimes the players didn't turn on her; they saved their venom for each other.

"Why did you take that card? If you didn't take that card, I would have won."

"You took the bust card. If you didn't take the bust card, we all would have won."

She liked it better when they fought among themselves than when they picked on her.

All the players weren't bad, sometimes they were pleasant or funny. A sweet older man with silver hair swept up into an Elvis-do pointed to a bet placed right above his. "This is for you, honey."

Customers were definitely not politically correct. She was addressed as honey, sweetie, baby, pretty girl, and other various forms of endearment throughout the night. Reluctantly, she admitted to herself she didn't care what they called her as long as they were tipping.

Customers made comments on her looks, her personality, and even her ethnicity. "You're a tall one aren't you," more than one asked, like maybe she had never noticed her own height.

"Oh look, Neil, she's white. We like the white dealers. They speak English."

At the end of the night John handed Caroline a steaming cup of hot chocolate before he sat across from her at a booth in the employee dining room. After offering that inscrutable smile, he laughed. "Well, how did it go? Are you ready to go to Indio and play?" Indio Springs was another casino down valley.

"You were right," she admitted without a qualm. "After one night of dealing, I swear I will never play at a blackjack table again. Every time I lost a toke bet I began to feel physically ill. All those tips down the drain. I lost way more than I won. I am mentally and physically exhausted. After standing for eight hours, my feet ache. I can't wait to kick off these shoes."

"Swollen feet. A hazard of the trade." He leaned back and settled in.

"After adding for eight hours, my mind is blank. I can't wait to go home and pour myself a large glass of wine. After dealing with the public for eight hours, I feel like a tree. The players say the rudest things while I just stand up straight and ignore them. I know why they call new dealers break-ins, I feel broken."

"You seem cool, calm and collected to me."

"I feel like a heap of dirty clothes lying on the bottom of my closet." She pinched a piece of fabric from her shirt, held it up to her nose, and sniffed. "And I smell like a cigarette in a brewery."

"As anyone who works with the public knows, people are the problem." He nodded his head in a gesture of empathy. "Soon it will all be like white noise in the background."

"But there was an outstanding outcome. I made this." She held up three big ones, crisp one-hundred-dollar bills. "You were right, dealing will be a great way to get out of debt. Tell me the truth, were Andrei and I as obnoxious as some of the people I dealt to tonight?"

"Nonsense, you were lovely. You two were excellent tippers, and that's all dealers care about."

She blew on her hot chocolate to cool it. "You're right. Life is funny, when I got into the management training program, I worried about how the dealers would react to me, especially since we sold some of them houses the banks foreclosed on. I apologized to everyone I ever sold a house to. Most of them just shrugged and said they blamed the banks, that the problems were bigger than all of us, and they were all just grateful to still have a job. They only shared one complaint. They were sorry to lose such a big tipper to the other side of the table. Excuse me, I have to do this." She kicked off her shoes and sighed in pleasure. "Relief."

After a long graveyard shift, she walked out of the casino to greet another bright sunny day because there is one thing you can bank on, the sun is going to shine in Palm Springs. At the time when most people were leaving for work, she was returning to her studio apartment. Still adjusting to living alone, the compact space made her feel safe. Her new home had been built in the forties as a hotel room with a tiny kitchenette and a fireplace for cold winter nights. Her life and her room were small, consisting of work and home.

In an attempt to pay off her fine to the IRS as soon as possible, she worked as many shifts as the bosses gave her. Once she entered her cocoon, she closed the blinds and switched on the television. She allowed herself only one luxury, a subscription to cable television. Like many broken women her life revolved around the "save me I'm dying" channel. Even though they were only works of fiction, she empathized with these women. She hated to admit it, but she was in a very dark place where the only thing that gave her joy was watching the suffering of others.

Chapter Fifteen

When Buying a Home, Always Take a Fixed Rate Mortgage

Caroline slid a piece of paper across the desk. A calm bespectacled man sitting on the opposite side picked it up. Glancing around the small bare bones office that smelled of disinfectant, she decided this man would never let himself fall into financial trouble. Miles Nickels, the accountant for the Shotowa Tribe for more than forty years, came highly recommended by John Tovar.

Embarrassed and knowing she sounded frantic, she blurted, "See this figure. It says I owe the IRS $187,695. I don't get it. All my property has been foreclosed on. I've declared bankruptcy. There is nothing left. How can I owe so much money?"

"If you don't mind, Ms. Popov, I will give you a lesson on how taxes work. You and your husband—" he read the name on the tax bill, "—Andrei took out two million dollars in loans. After the bank foreclosed on the properties, they sold the properties in short sales. Your debt was relieved because you live in California, and once there is a short sale here, you have no further obligation on the mortgage. But here's the catch, the banks sold the properties for less than you owed on your mortgage. You owe taxes on the difference. The government considers that money income."

"Income?" she yelped. "I made nothing. I have nothing."

Mr. Nickels never blinked. "For example, you bought a property for four hundred thousand dollars, and the bank sold it for two hundred thousand. You are taxed on the two hundred thousand dollars the bank lost. The IRS considers it a capital gain for you. I have more bad news. Since you used the money you borrowed to purchase investment property and not for a primary residence, you can't cancel the tax liability in bankruptcy. Multiply back taxes on four more properties and you have a bill for..." He glanced at the amount. "$187,695."

"Oh my God." Her heart pounded so hard she feared her chest would explode.

"Maybe we can settle with the IRS, knock the amount down. I know a few top-notch tax lawyers."

"Great. More lawyers, just what I need. I can barely afford you."

"Believe me, good advice from a professional is exactly what you need. I will give you their phone numbers. But first let me share one piece of unsolicited advice—if you ever consider property in the future, only buy it if you can make the payments on a thirty-year fixed loan. No adjustable, no interest only, or any other kind of crazy loan the banks make up, only fixed interest. I hope I never have to deliver this speech again."

His words stung and his tone was a bit harsh. "I wished you had been advising us before we borrowed all that money."

But now the damage was done, and she realized that for the next several years she needed to make more money, lots of money. Luckily, she worked in the casino money store, and to get some of that money, she needed to figure out how to maximize her earning potential. The fastest way to achieve her goal was to become the best dealer because everyone knew the best dealer wasn't the one who dealt the fastest or cleanest game, but the one who made the most tips. The amount she owed the IRS seemed so enormous she found it hard to wrap her head around it. The meeting over, Miles escorted her to the door and shook her hand.

****

At the end of the graveyard shift, the dealers gathered at Slaherty's, the fake Irish pub near the casino. At that hour, their only company professional alcoholics who sat across from them at the bar.

Once they settled into their stools, Caroline turned her attention to the savvy redhead perched beside her. This woman was a legend on the casino floor because she had elevated tip making into a scientific formula. "Abigail, I've been watching you engage the customers so effortlessly. Every time I glance over at your table, your players are always laughing. You make more tips than any dealer on our shift, and I want to know how you do it because I need to make a lot of money, yesterday."

She could tell Abigail was flattered by the compliment. "Most people say you have to be a gambler to make money dealing. I disagree, you just have to know how gamblers think. Gamblers believe they are a little smarter than everybody else. Learn to play into their vanity. They thrive on praise. Compliment the decisions they make at the table."

She pitched her voice higher and smiled. "Mr.

Kennedy, doubling down on eleven was brilliant. I can sum up my strategy for you. Always be upbeat. Feed their vanity like you did mine. Carry on a running conversation with the players. It's pretty much that simple. When a stiff sits at my table I take it as a challenge to see if I can turn him into a tipper. Here, give me your hands." She rubbed Caroline's hands. "I just rubbed some of my luck on you, to show support."

Heeding the advice, Caroline transformed herself into a puppet on a string. Pushing into a blackjack game, she greeted the customers in a loud hearty voice because a good dealer learns to project their voice in order to compete with the background noise of the casino. Also to be successful, she should be able to read a player's preferences. If the player was a Democrat, she became a Democrat. If a customer's favorite football team was Seattle, "What a great game last night. The Seahawks crushed it." Memorizing the daily sports scores came in handy.

Keeping current on books and movies also helped and being able to recommend local restaurants always scored points. "Have you tried the new French bistro on Palm Canyon, their quiche is to die for." Her goal was to turn a player into a friend. She cheered every time her players won a hand and cried with them when they lost. She laughed at jokes that weren't funny. She became the perfect chameleon, and tips began to flow into her box.

The more the players bet, the higher the tips. So the high limit games were her gold mines. When Ray, her favorite player, began winning, she teased him, "I've been so generous to you. I must be your favorite dealer." What she really meant was, you've won a lot of money, you should be throwing some of it my way. Then she did a really cheesy thing, she winked. It worked, Ray bet a green for her, a twenty-five-dollar chip. If he won, then she won also and earned fifty dollars. Who wouldn't cheer for that?

Immediately an over enthusiastic high pitched giddy, "Thank you," escaped from her practiced lips, pitched loud enough so the other players on the table could hear. When Ray won the hand, she sighed a huge sigh of relief and tapped her two winning green chips loudly on the table before she dropped them into her locked tip box.

This spurred the British man on spot five to put up his own chip for her. "Thank you so much," she gushed.

Getting a Brit to tip, icing on the cake. Since they weren't known for generosity, she would happily teach them the American way. People liked to show off to the dealer and the people around them. It wasn't unusual for players to compete to see who could fill up her tip box the fastest, especially once they learned she kept her own tips, no sharing. Her favorite players were Asian, Chinese, and Koreans because they believed tipping led to good luck, and she encouraged their superstitions.

Emotionally crushed and defeated after returning from her disastrous cruise to Russia, her initial plan had been to come home, declare bankruptcy, and return their properties back to the bank. Free of debt, she would triumphantly return to St. Petersburg, and bring Andrei home. Old pop songs familiar to all generations were always playing when she worked. Most of the time the music was part of the background haze, but each morning around dawn when the casino was quiet, she would hear Mike and the Mechanics sing about needing a miracle. At first the song made her hopeful, but after a few months of pushing cards across the table, it began to feel like the words were taunting her. She realized there would be no miracle, just hard work. It would take years to pay off their debt.

She vowed to go home that morning and build a fire so she could watch her romance novels burn. Romance novels lied. In a story when people owed money, it magically appeared. In the real world, money mostly disappeared. She prayed for an inheritance from a relative she never met, but she knew all her relatives, and none of them had money.

Discovering they were bankrupt was like being diagnosed with a chronic disease she would have to live with for the rest of her life. She suffered through the five stages of grief. On the way home from Russia, she tried to convince herself that things couldn't really be as dire as Andrei said—classic first stage denial. But then she returned home and met with the bank manager and an accountant. On some days she allowed herself to be honest, to admit she was angry—stage two. Andrei had ruined their lives and she didn't understand why he couldn't come home and face the music. Over Skype she tried to bargain with him to no avail, promising him, even though the road to becoming whole would be hard, together they could overcome anything. But pride stood in his way. Instead of working with her, he deserted her. If he truly loved her, he would have come back. She fell into depression. She was on her own, only now saddled with an enormous debt to pay.

On Valentine's Day, arriving home to her bleak

studio apartment after work, the blinking answering machine greeted her. Expecting a sales call, preparing to ignore it, she glanced down at the caller ID. The country code blinked Russia. She ran to grab it, fearing that something bad had happened to Andrei.

Hands shaking, she clicked the voicemail, and the distressed voice of Andrei's mother filled the room. "I believe my son is on the verge of breaking down. I know no way to make him leave his bed. Last night he refused my borscht, his favorite food." The news broke Caroline's heart all over again.

"He could make new start in Russia if he cut ties to you, but he refuses. Please, Caroline, either come back to St. Petersburg or cut him free. Remember, it is easier for the mare when a woman gets off the cart."

Stung from the rebuke from his mother while fearing for his sanity, she decided to let Andrei's calls go to voice mail. She couldn't bear to change her number—she loved hearing the sound of his voice—but she wouldn't allow herself to speak to him, only listen.

"I'm sorry, I'm sorry. Please forgive me. I love you." Thousands of miles apart from each other, they both existed in a state of purgatory. He cried, then she cried alone at the sound of his voice. Finally she arrived at the last stage of grief—acceptance.

Somehow, she would break her ties to Andrei. A ridiculous plan entered her mind. She needed to sleep with someone else and then confess her sin, confident that after the ultimate betrayal, Andrei would surely dump her. He had been so proud he had been her first and only lover, so in her twisted state of mind, she reasoned that if she took away their bond, it would lead to the end of this hell. No obvious candidates came to mind, but she was sure there were plenty of dealers or customers who would happily oblige. However, working as a management trainee sleeping with co-workers was not a wise idea and sleeping with customers an even worse one.

Living in Palm Springs where gays and lesbians made up half of the population meant the pickings were slim for heterosexual women. But there was one bar, Zena, a local institution, a quick walk from her small studio apartment where all the tourists on the prowl would eventually end up. She reminded herself she just needed one person.

Abigail was always pleading with her to go out because, "We need to find some fellas."

Caroline reminded her, "I found a fella, and it broke me."

The next weekend she surprised Abigail by agreeing to go to Zena. In preparation she pulled her Murphy bed down from the wall before she left the apartment.

Abigail pushed them ahead of the line of tourists waiting at the door. At first the club intimidated Caroline—a cavernous room, vibrating from the music pouring out of booming speakers. After a few minutes she realized that the night club really didn't seem much different from the casino, except smoking wasn't allowed, making the air clearer.

Her friend scanned the room, disco balls hung from the ceiling and strobe lights pulsed through the room, adding to the retro feel. "I've checked out some great possibilities here. Let's get some drinks. We need some liquid courage."

Standing at the bar a tall, dark-haired stranger

offered to buy them a drink, but he resembled Andrei too closely. She wanted to forget her husband, not sleep with his double. Awkwardly jostling through the crowd, out of the corner of her eye she spotted a friend from college, actually an old crush, talking and drinking with a group of guys at the bar. She gathered up her courage and tentatively approached him. "Dylan, I haven't seen you in ages."

He fixed his gaze on her. "You look fantastic!"

"Flattery will get you everywhere." Could adultery be this easy? Caroline wondered. Less than five minutes have elapsed since I walked in the door and spied an old crush I never thought I would see again— mission accomplished.

Dylan was a handsome man. His strawberry blond hair contrasted nicely with his tan. Under the disco lights his freckles lit up as he smiled. His smile conveyed the confidence of someone who had thrived since college. "What brings you to the desert?" she asked blithely.

"Guys' golf weekend. Why Palm Springs? Because this is the best place in the world to play golf. My fraternity used to come down here for Spring Break; we played all weekend. Now, every year we hold a mini reunion. Let me introduce you to the guys."

The next few minutes were filled with names, faces, and shaking hands. When Dylan held the glass in the air, she couldn't help but notice the ring on his hand, the first hiccup in her plans.

She wondered if she could go against her morals and sleep with someone else's husband. The bigger question was could she sleep with a golfer? Golfers were the most obnoxious customers at the casino, smug and self-absorbed. They tended to brag about how rich they were while at the same time avoiding tipping. Experience had taught her that whenever someone bragged about how rich they were, you better not expect a tip. *Well, maybe I can sleep with one golfer. Dylan probably isn't rich.*

A few shots later her logic became fuzzier. Dylan pulled out his cell phone to show her his screen saver, a picture of his daughter. "She is the love of my life." He never mentioned his wife. Maybe he wasn't happy. She only wanted to borrow him for a night, not break up a marriage.

When he took her hand in his leading her onto the dance floor, an unexpected jolt of electricity passed through her. Negotiating their space across the crowded dance floor, he held her close and whispered in her ear, "Why didn't we get together in college?"

A rare slow mournful song began to fill the room. Even though she willed it away, a picture of Andrei passed through her head. Whenever the Scorpions sang about the changes in Russia, Andrei became excited because it was the story of the breaking apart of his country. In Dylan's arms, the realization hit her hard, she couldn't follow through with her plan. With romance out of the picture, the night morphed into a pleasant reunion with an old friend.

Later, shooting yet another shot of tequila with old and new friends, she experienced an aha moment. She didn't have to sleep with Dylan, only convince Andrei she did. Although it wouldn't be easy, she would lie. She would keep the back story but change Dylan's name to protect the innocent. Instantly she relaxed, and the rest of the night passed pleasantly as she and

Abigail danced and partied with a group of golfers from Long Beach who, contrary to her belief, happened to be pretty nice guys.

Chapter Sixteen

In Cards as in Romance, Once a Cheater, Always a Cheater

Walking through the blackjack pit, dressed in a designer suit was a new sensation for Caroline. She had recently been promoted to floor supervisor. Now her job was to keep track of the games, approve markers and fills, correct the dealer's mistakes, and most importantly, catch cheaters. In her first few weeks she realized that she wasn't the only dealer who made mistakes. Everyone paid pushes, hit the wrong hands, or accidentally picked up winners. Now, she made the calls, the decisions about how to fix mistakes and keep the customers happy.

Each game had a screen attached at the side. Sophisticated new software kept track of the money and the players. John made big plans for her, and she was thrilled to oblige. For some strange reason she loved working in the casino. The place was filled with so many derelicts she didn't feel like such a screwup. She enjoyed the challenge of being a manager and learning new skills. There might be some dull moments but never a dull day.

Because each floor person supervised four games, she split her time walking the pit, watching each of her games. Excited because Abigail was dealing in her section tonight, she stopped behind her game knowing it would be entertaining. She worried it might be hard to manage the people she worked with for years, but so far so good. Taking inventory of her tables she noticed four regulars, bartenders who worked at the Parma Casino down valley gambling at Abigail's table.

Her players were laughing and drinking while her tip box was filling up with chips. "Let's make some money," she yelled before she dealt out each hand.

Filling up a tip box might seem easy, but it was hard work. First the player had to win some money so they felt like a winner—plus, winning provided an incentive to tip. Next the dealer had to win her tips, a hard task since everyone knows the odds are with the house.

Abigail hit out her hand and busted with a twenty-two. The guys had placed four five-dollar tip bets for her in front of their bets. Caroline was genuinely happy her friend would make forty dollars. She watched her pay the bet at third base and then push her tip bet out, sliding her finger across the top of the chips to verify the payout to the cameras. Abigail repeated the payouts until the bets were all paid and then picked up her bets, tapped them twice against the table to signal to the cameras that these were tips, and dropped them in her tip box. The box clinked eight times as the chips hit the bottom.

Caroline glimpsed a sliver of green between the red of the chips. That's funny, there were only five dollars bets out for the dealer. Did Abigail make a mistake? Did she accidentally mix a green chip in with her red chips and drop an extra twenty-five dollars in her box? Not wanting to disturb the game, Caroline decided to call surveillance to have them review the tape. If Abigail had made a mistake, she would retrieve the money from her tip box and put it back in the rack.

At the end of the shift her cell phone buzzed. The casino manager wanted to see her *right now*. She climbed up the stairs to the manager's office, wondering where she screwed up and how much money she'd cost the casino.

In the office John and the Casino Manager Jerry, a tough old guy who worked his way up through the poker rooms of California, waited for her. Tension as thick as smoke from a cigar hung in the air.

John spoke first, "Sometimes this is a hard job and we have to make hard choices. You did right to call surveillance on Abigail."

Confused, Caroline stared at them. "I never got a call back. I was sure I made a mistake."

"Today you just got your first dealer fired. After surveillance started watching the tapes, they discovered Abigail has been stealing. She slipped a green into her box. They then pulled the tapes of her dealing for the last month. It's easy to do that now, the new software prints out a report every night of what games the dealers dealt on."

"How stupid." Caroline was angry. "She is well aware whenever a dealer taps into a game and places their index finger over the scanner she is being tracked. She knows the program records the name of the dealer, the time, and the number of the game into a database."

"Surveillance reported multiple instances where a green chip accidentally found its way into her box," Jerry explained. "She palmed those chips like a magician. You must have excellent eyesight because apparently, she has been getting away with this for years. I guess she got away with stealing for so long she believed she was invincible. But we both know I have to fire her. I am disappointed. I really liked that girl." Jerry ended his speech with a sigh.

"I can't believe she steals," Caroline said. "She was my mentor, taught me how to deal."

"But your first loyalty has to be to the casino," Jerry added. "Remember, stealing puts the heat on the other dealers. She wasn't looking out for their welfare, or yours either; she could have gotten you in real trouble."

"But she made so much money from tips she didn't have to steal."

"She didn't have to, she wanted to," Jerry emphasized his point. "Watching the tapes, surveillance became suspicious of her because she was always glancing around the casino as she dealt, not concentrating on her game. In the future, remember, always watch the dealer who is watching you. We need you to write an incident report about what you saw." He handed her a writeup form. "Make sure you don't breathe a word of this to anyone. This might help. We're giving you a one-hundred and fifty-dollar gift certificate for the Steak House. Great job."

"I don't have anyone to take to dinner," she said, "because I just got my best friend fired."

Chapter Seventeen

Twentynine Palms, California, September 2019

Making her way through the casino, Caroline spotted the familiar sight of Holly the astrology lady perched at her favorite machine, merrily pulling the handles, while consulting astrology charts on her smart phone, searching for her lucky moment. She got Holly a cup of coffee, delivering it with a smile. "Special Delivery. I thought you might need a pick me up."

"Thanks, I need some of your magic." Holly rested the cup on the ledge of her machine and held out both hands.

Caroline began to rub her hands. "Okay, now win a big one." Her cell phone vibrated. "I would love to stay and chat, but you know, duty calls."

She made her way over to Jesus Gonzales, the slots manager, who stood in front of a bank of slot machines. "Let's move over here. Be discreet." He directed her to a spot on the casino floor where they could speak without being overheard. "See, those two guys at the dollar machines? From the pile of incident reports on my desk, I can see they've been doing some shady stuff, putting thousands of dollars into the machine, playing one or two hands, and then cashing out."

Two short, black-haired men, dressed in loose gauzy cotton shirts and jeans, stood at a machine, sliding cash into the bill acceptor. They held stacks of bills in their opposite hands.

"Do you think they've mistaken the casino for a laundromat?" she asked.

As a manager, one of the first things she became aware of was the amount of money laundered through casinos, up to a mind boggling two trillion dollars a year. People came loaded with dirty money made from illegal activities and cleaned it by running it through the casino dry cleaner. Inquisitive, she tried not to stare in their direction. "Do you know who they are?"

"According to their players' cards, the one on the left is Assam Kazem, and the one on the right is Hassan Yusuf," Jesus said. "They have been playing here for the last few weeks. In the last few days their cash play has really picked up. What do you want me to do?"

"File a suspicious activity report. Report to me if they do anything else fishy."

"Will do, boss," Jesus replied. "I'll keep my eye on them. You can depend on me."

Later in the shift, Ann Allen called Caroline to the blackjack pit. Ann, a slim brownette, replaced Derrick Thomas as table games manager. Caroline had broken in with her at the Palm Oasis, and she liked her work. More importantly, she trusted her.

Standing at the podium in the middle of the pit, Ann scanned an incident report displayed on the computer terminal. "I have some suspicious activity to report to you," she said, jerking her chin toward her left. "I have a player over there at the high limit blackjack table, sitting on third base. His name is Justin. I believe he is an officer at the Marine base, but it's hard to know because he won't tell us his last name. For the last month he has played here almost every night. Sometimes he's alone, usually a few buddies come with him. When he thinks I'm not watching, he passes hundred-dollar chips to his pals who then exchange the chips for cash."

"You're right," Caroline agreed. "That is suspicious."

"That isn't the only thing that is suspicious. Follow me." They walked over to the high limit table. Wearing thick glasses, the man known as Justin acted more like a tech geek than a solider. He wore the buzz cut of a Marine and carried the demeanor of a college professor. Instead of smoking a pipe, he vaped on a pen, exhaling the sweet smell of cherry in a puff of water vapor. A horrible habit, in Caroline's opinion, but a step more tolerable than smoking tobacco. When the dealer paused at the end of the hand, Justin pulled out a wad of cash, laying it down on the table.

Ann addressed the dealer, "Kim, could you give us a minute. I need to talk to Justin." She then looked at him. "You are reaching a threshold. You can't cash out any more money tonight unless you give me your identification."

He stuffed his money back into his pocket. "Guess it's time for me to take a break and grab some dinner. See you later." He stood and walked away from the table.

The women walked back over to the podium. According to the information on Ann's computer station, Justin was close to reaching the daily limit of ten thousand dollars. If a player cashed in a penny more than the limit allowed by the Internal Revenue Service, the casino had to fill out a CTR, a Currency Transaction

Report.

"This is the exact opposite of what just happened at the slot machines," Caroline said. "It's apparent this Justin guy doesn't want to cross the threshold. And his play certainly qualifies as suspicious, so fill out an SAR." Suspicious Activity Reports followed the money.

Ann typed away on the computer. "Players try to delude themselves that by choosing a small casino in the back of beyond they can get away with some underhanded stuff."

"But they underestimate the dynamic duo. You and me." Caroline gave a thumbs up. "Call me if he returns." Her cell phone began to vibrate. "Guess it's time to put out the next fire."

Chapter Eighteen

If You Walk Into a Casino, You Are on Camera

"How am I supposed to act? What do I call him? I've never met a general before."

Earlier, John notified Caroline of an emergency meeting with General Brisson, commander of the base at Twentynine Palms, adding that it was top secret. "Just call him General Brisson. He's a great guy, a regular Marine." Never once as an enlisted man did he imagine he would be hosting a two star major general.

"Is this related to the suspicious activity report the casino filed on the guy named Justin? I hope he's not annoyed at us for reporting one of his officers."

In order to keep the meeting private, it was held at midnight on a Tuesday in a hotel events room, usually reserved for weddings and business conferences and far from the casino floor. John and Brisson decided to arrive in disguises of matching flannel shirts and baseball caps, via a service entrance. It might be a bit over the top but a man in the uniform of a US Marine general would attract unwanted attention.

Entering, they noticed a screen had been set up, and a projector positioned on the conference table. They overheard Joanna talking to Caroline as she fiddled with the screen. "We will play the message, and then the tape will self-destruct, leaving no trace."

Caroline laughed. "This is going to be fun."

As the two men walked into the room, a flustered Ann joined them, shutting the door behind her. "Hope I haven't missed anything."

John shook his head. "We're just starting. General Brisson, I would like to introduce Ann Allen, the table games manager. She brought the suspicious activity to our attention." He then proceeded to go around the table, introducing everyone else. "Caroline Popov is our casino manager. Beside her is Brandon Boyd, he handles security at the Night Hawk, and Joanna Tovar, head of surveillance."

Years ago, when John had first met Brisson, he had been surprised to see a short, bald man, age somewhere between fifty and sixty, he found it hard to gauge his exact age. He didn't fit the stereotype of a general but then he spoke. "Ms. Popov, Ms. Tovar, Ms. Allen and Mr. Boyd, it is a pleasure to meet you." His deep, clear, strong voice sounded like someone used to being in command.

Introductions over, Brisson spoke to the group. "I know you are wondering why we are here." He stopped, glanced at the tips of his shiny shoes, then back up. "When FinCEN calls and informs you that the Night Hawk has been tracking the activities of a high roller whom they believe to be a US Marine, that is a call I have to take seriously. You don't mess with the IRS." Everyone in the room knew FinCEN was the investigative unit of the Internal Revenue Service.

John injected a note of caution. "I couldn't agree more. According to the Bank Secrecy Act, FinCEN has the ability to shut the Night Hawk down. Even though we are a sovereign nation we have to follow federal laws. General Brisson, our team has been hard at work gathering evidence. Joanna, I think it is time to get on with the show."

Brandon walked over to the wall and flipped a switch, shutting off the lights. All eyes in the darkened room focused on the screen. Images of Justin gambling at a blackjack table, chips spread in front of him, were projected on the screen. Two guys stood behind him.

Joanna explained, "Over the past week, since the original report was filed, we've kept a camera on Justin, recording all his activities. I don't think you want to watch all forty hours of his play. Instead, we condensed the video data into one highlight reel of his greatest hits. Sort of like a movie trailer, where they spoil it by showing you all the best parts of the movie."

For the next ten minutes they watched their suspect play cards. If he lost, he traded cash in for chips. If he won, he passed winning chips to his buddies. She froze the screen.

Speaking quickly, Ann took over the narration. "The player in the center goes by the name Justin. He's downstairs at a blackjack table right now. He says he works at Twentynine Palms but refuses to give us his identification. He's been coming into the casino for the last month, buys in with amounts just shy of ten thousand dollars. General, you probably don't know this but a player can only cash in nine thousand nine hundred and ninety-nine dollars in one day, not a penny more. This Justin always stops before we have to fill out a transaction currency report, which we would have to report to the IRS. Am I making myself clear?"

Brisson nodded. "I'm learning. Continue."

Anne spoke very quickly. "A casino can pick any

time to end their reporting day. We choose to end our reporting day at midnight. He can cash in more money after midnight because it is technically the start of a new reporting day. He gambles like he's not really worried about losing the money, like there's more where that came from. I think he knows when our reporting day ends because he comes in with more cash after midnight." Ann paused and glanced down at her notes.

John broke in. "Ann, do many Marines gamble like this?"

"No, this behavior is highly unusual, most Marines gamble less than five hundred dollars. Sometimes he hands chips to his friends at the table, and they cash them out. Even though he didn't technically exceed the limit, he obviously doesn't understand that much unreported money passing through the casino, day after day, doesn't look good and we're required to report it." Ann let out a breath, like she was glad to be finished.

Caroline had been fidgeting in her seat, waiting for her turn to speak. "I know those two guys sitting beside him. They've been playing at the slots. And *playing* is a very loose term. They have been putting large amounts of money into the machines. I don't know if the money they are playing is dirty, but once they put it through the machines it comes out clean."

Brisson removed his baseball cap and ran a hand over his regulation buzz cut of steel gray hair. "Thanks for the explanation, ma'am. His real name is Justin, last name Riskin. He's a ground supply officer, in charge of purchasing and contracting supplies for the base. He also develops the spending plans. The other two, Hassan and Assam, work at the Middle Eastern village we built at the base. We use it to train enlisted men, about life in an Arab village. Their job is to teach soldiers rudimentary language, how to adhere to the customs, the things that can save their life. We transfer people here from the Middle East who worked with us. Those two translated for me in Syria."

Brisson shook his head. "I'm not sure where Justin gets his money, but it is a sure thing he's not gambling on a Marine's salary. But what are the other two doing?"

Joanna switched off the projector. "In surveillance we see this all the time. They are laundering his money. They put it into a slot machine play a few hands, cash out and print out a receipt. Then using that receipt, they can claim the money as winnings. Once it is laundered, they can legally deposit it into a bank account. They just need to keep their receipts from the casino. Although these days they could just as easily bypass a bank and buy crypto currency."

John strived to reassure the general. "If these guys are breaking the law, I have a great team here. We'll catch them."

"Maybe this will help," Ann said. "Justin told me he worked with computers. I asked about the best brand to buy for my middle school daughter. He offered to sell me a computer at an unbelievably low price, claimed it was Marine surplus. Common sense told me it wasn't acceptable to buy something from a guest because it felt too much like a bribe. I politely rejected his offer."

"Thanks, for the information," Bisson said. "Now, we have to catch him in the act."

Caroline said, "We'll make a movie, but we will be

the only ones that know that we are filming. We'll keep tracking what he's doing, film the evidence, and give it to you, General Brisson." Ever since they had taken down Derrick, she was dying to be involved with another sting.

John hesitated. He didn't want to place anyone in danger. "Maybe we should let the Marines handle this."

"No really," she insisted. "I swear we can do this, it will all be on tape, and we never have to leave the casino. Look at the screen with its gritty dark interior, sleazy subject matter, and smoky atmosphere. It plays like a film noir. Joanna already runs surveillance on him whenever he walks into the casino. We're all on camera all the time anyway. Don't let her talent go to waste."

Brandon backed her up. "John, I have complete confidence in Ms. Popov. Let's listen to what she says."

"First I need him to trust me," Caroline said, then went on to propose her plan. "When he does, I'll ask him if he knows where I can get a good computer. I'll set the trap, he'll take the bait, and I'll reel him in."

John disagreed. He loved playing cops and robbers but this crossed a line. "The femme fatale, absolutely not. I don't want to put you in danger. Remember the billboard incident."

Caroline snapped, "That was months ago. Nothing has happened since. It was just someone trying to scare me, and it didn't work." She glared at John. "You made me casino manager, so let me manage. Let me find out what is going on with Justin before he implicates any of my employees in a crime. I don't want anyone to lose their job because they trusted the wrong person." As an afterthought, she pulled the gender card. "If I were a man, you'd have no problems with this plan."

Joanna added, "You are always saying how important your employees are."

He knew it was true. He treated Caroline with kid gloves because she was a woman, but he didn't want his sexism to hold her back from fulfilling her potential. "I guess the guys don't get to have all the fun. You play dirty, I can't resist the noir theme. Okay, fill me in. If General Brisson agrees."

Brisson gave a thumbs-up. "You know if we can use the resources of the casino I agree with Caroline, this seems like a doable plan. I'll agree on the condition that you give me a copy of the movie. I can use it as evidence."

John's enthusiasm grew. "I want to be involved every step of the way."

Caroline consulted notes she'd scribbled on a napkin. "Of course, you have a big part in this movie. Who else could play the wisecracking private detective? Besides, if Joanna, our director, ever senses I am in danger, she can send in the hero, Brandon, who will lurk in the shadows to save me from the outsider, Justin. With dozens of security guards guarding this place I feel pretty safe, and as I promised I'll never leave the building with him." She put down her napkin and spoke to the general. "And for the finale, the Marines will be waiting off screen ready to arrest him."

"I'm gonna make a movie," Joanna yelled in triumph. "My dream come true."

After everyone returned to work and only John and General Brisson remained in the room, John pulled a couple cigars from the top pocket of his flannel shirt. "Let's enjoy some of these beauties. They aren't real

Cubans but they were rolled by real Cubans in Miami's Little Havana." He handed the general a cigar. "I am sure you have some fascinating stories about life at the base, and I would love to hear them."

The two men lit their cigars, and as the smell of burnt fog filled the air, they settled down for a long bullshit session.

Chapter Nineteen

To Be Successful a Casino Needs to Integrate into the Community

"Look up here, we're on television." Deanna pointed at the screen hanging from the ceiling in the breakroom. "And for once it's not for some scandal. Shh, everyone, after the commercial Stephanie Ramirez is going to interview John."

"Oh damn, I'm late."

Caroline had been passing through the employee lounge. She exited to the parking lot on her way to the art fair. Since the days were still unbearably hot, Marketing had decided to hold the event at night to take advantage of the fact that low humidity cools the desert down after sunset. She took her place on a small stage filled with local dignitaries.

John stood talking to a pretty brunette from a Los Angeles TV affiliate. "We are very excited to host the first monthly Night of the Arts. It is our opportunity to let the many talented people in this valley show us what they've got. We will be showcasing local artists and restaurants. Come for the art and stay for the food." His charisma ratio dialed to full force, he worked hard to make this night a success. Caroline imagined all the women who, after watching him on their TV screens, canceled any plans, getting into their cars and driving to the Night Hawk, hoping to meet the handsome Chairman Tovar.

Stephanie Ramirez spoke directly into the camera, "As you can see crowd is growing. For a good time, take the advice of the Shotowa Tribal Chairman, John Tovar, and come on down." Behind her crowds lined up at the food trucks. A Native American band began to play indigenous music. New Age harmonies heavy on flutes and rattles filled the air.

The High Desert was gaining national attention as a mecca for artists escaping Los Angeles. Most of the locals welcomed the newcomers but every once in a while, she would spot someone wearing a *go back to LA* T-shirt in the casino. But opportunities to sell art in the desert were limited. When the local artists cooperative approached Caroline about starting the festival, she was thrilled for a chance to do something positive for the community. At the same time it would give people who didn't gamble a chance to visit the Night Hawk. In a small town like Twentynine Palms, the casino acted like the town center and the village green combined.

After the interview John spoke to Caroline, "Let's check out the merchandise. It will be fun to wander the fair like any other tourist."

The parking lot had been transformed into a wonderland. A full moon lit the sky, silhouetting the majestic mountains in the background. Iron sculptures of extinct dinosaurs and wooly mammoths that once roamed the land had been scattered around the fair. The theme was *The Eternal Land.* Booths of artists displaying their wares were set up, illuminated by strings of sparkling fairy lights.

They passed by booths selling surrealistic paintings of dragons and serpents playing in the desert. Glazed pottery that seemed like it had been thrown from the red clay of the surrounding hills were arranged in front of a kiln where fair goers could try their hand at throwing a pot. Glass blowers bent brightly colored orbs of glass into the shapes of birds, trees, and flowers of the desert.

Their progress was slow because every few steps they were interrupted by players and employees wanting to talk to John. He greeted everyone enthusiastically. Waiting, she occupied herself with snapping photos and sending them to Mindy via her phone.

Happily, John posed for selfies with his adoring fans. When she was snapping a photo of him with a Dutch couple, who had never met a real Native American chief, she realized he suffered from the need to please. A serious person, she realized his striving to make everybody happy would be the exact reason she would never want to be in a romantic relationship with him. He thrived on the approval of many women. One would never be enough. She wanted, *always only you.*

"I see Holly's booth. Let's get her to tell our fortunes." Caroline had recruited her to add an air of mystery to the event.

Once inside, Holly led her to a table. She held Caroline's open palm, taking time to study the lines and creases. "You have earth hands, which means that you are practical and grounded. Your fate line shows that you have come out of a very challenging time, but your heart line is long. I predict that you will love again." She pointed to a line that intersected her hand. "I also see a tall handsome man beside you."

John laughed. "You must mean me."

After the reading, Caroline checked out Holly's booth. Dozens of statues lined the shelves. Picking up a ceramic of a chubby Buddha, a beatific smile plastered on his face, she commented to Holly, "You really do love the Buddha."

"That one is especially lucky. What can I say, I am Catholic but these little guys have always been lucky for me. What is your lucky charm?"

Leaving, she turned to Holly. "I'll let you know, when I figure it out."

John pulled her toward the food trucks. "I'm starving. Let's go eat before the food is all gone."

"This is so delicious," Caroline gushed over their bison burgers, served with truffle fries. "John, I think you are my lucky charm. You may not realize it but when you offered me a job I could barely get up in the morning. I felt like a total failure, both personally and professionally. Sometimes when you're down you feel like you don't deserve anything, but then you stepped in and changed my life. You didn't just give me a job, you gave me an identity."

"That's right, you're my Casino Queen," he said, with a smile in his eyes. "One of the ten commandments of the Shotowa nation is to give assistance and kindness whenever needed."

"I'm not ashamed to admit, I needed assistance, but I appreciated the kindness more. Little by little, I got caught up in all the challenges of the job and started looking forward to coming to work. The mechanics of being able to pitch cards that didn't fly off the table appealed to me. When I learned to cut chips, I felt like a rock star. The casino was always filled with people, that meant I never had to be alone. I even loved the gossip. I'm just glad that now we can pay it forward. Great movie, very underrated."

"Confession over? I hate to admit it, but your words mean a lot to me."

By the time they returned to the fair, a crowd of high schoolers, checking each other out, had gathered around a local graffiti artist creating a painting holding cans of spray paint in each hand. So many of the artists were customers at the casino. She made it a point to stop by their booths and give them a word of encouragement. Sampling some home baked cinnamon rolls, she spotted the artist she had been searching for.

Rafi Nasser, an elfin slender man from Yemen with brilliant forest green eyes, was a genius jewelry designer who happened to be married to one of the Night Hawk's dealers, as she watched him wrap a gold necklace in silver crepe paper, she was reminded every piece of jewelry his wife wore was custom designed by him. Caroline waited patiently eyeing the beautiful pieces displayed behind glass cases and hanging from stands.

When his customer left, he greeted them with a nose kiss, he touched their noses with his. "Caroline and Chairman Tovar, how wonderful to see you. Peace be upon you. Thanks so much for putting on all this." A man who talked with his hands he threw his arms in the air. "Enjoy my work."

She had made a promise to herself to buy a necklace once her debt had been paid, to remind her of how much she had accomplished and sacrificed. "I want you to make me a necklace. I want it to be my lucky charm."

"In the Middle East we have the hamsa to ward off the evil eye. I just sold one when you walked up." He pointed to some pieces of jewelry that resembled an upside-down hand with a blue eye in the palms.

"I love those," Caroline said, "but I also love the number seven, and owls, they are sacred to the Shotowa. I can't decide."

John chimed in, "Don't forget the Queen of Hearts. That's who you are, and you made your own luck."

Rami opened a pad. "Why don't I make you a pendant incorporating all of those symbols, so you can be extra lucky." He drew out a piece of paper and, collaborating, they designed a square pendant.

She studied the drawing and declared, "I love it. Can you make it in rose gold? Do you promise you will never make another one like it?"

"Every piece I make is unique. Let's sprinkle gemstones through it, to make it sparkle in the light. It will take me about a week. Let's talk about payment and delivery."

Caroline spent the rest of the night elated by her purchase. After years of paying the IRS first, denying herself everything that wasn't absolutely necessary, she planned to spoil herself. With her job she really needed a lucky charm, especially if she was going to play undercover cop. She appreciated the irony of collaborating with her nemesis, the IRS. Life was funny that way, but today she would be satisfied that she didn't have to fire anyone or handle complaints from unhappy customers, she almost felt like a regular person.

Chapter: Twenty

Wins at the Casino Over Twenty-Five Hundred Dollars Should be Reported to the IRS

Caroline took a week to soften up a taciturn Justin by stalking, then luring him into her trap using all her best tipping strategies. On Saturday night, a few minutes before midnight, she plopped down beside him at the blackjack table. His hand consisted of two aces, which he split into two separate hands.

"What a great idea to split those aces," she said, complimenting him on his strategy, all the while breathing in his carcinogenic aerosol vape smoke. "Always split your aces and eights." Screaming with glee when he won, she said, "With smart players like you, how do we stay in business?"

She picked up her phone when it rang. "Laying it on pretty thick, Mata Hari," Joanna joked from her perch up in surveillance where she watched all the action.

"Glad that you are enjoying the show," Caroline said and ended the call. Her cheeks burned. She might be rusty when it came to using her feminine wiles, but she was prepared to pull out all the stops.

Then she baited the hook. "Justin, would you like to join me tomorrow night at the Chop House? We like to spoil our red card players."

He seemed delighted. "I'd love to, ma'am."

"Don't call me 'ma'am.' Caroline is fine. Is eight p.m. all right with you? I'll meet you at the bar just inside." Before she walked away, she winked at him. Cheesy but effective, she realized when he blushed.

The next night, ten minutes before her dinner date, she strategized with John and Brandon at the bar. Brandon dressed in street clothes, to blend in with the crowd. They were meeting in order to firm up their plans. True to form, things never ran smoothly in a casino.

Her cell phone rang. Mindful that casino business took priority over detective work, she turned to John. "I told Ann not to call me unless it is an emergency. This must be something important. Can you keep Justin busy till I get back?"

"I'll entertain him with old loudmouth." He patted a bottle of Cognac beside him at the bar. "That would make a dead man talk."

"Just make sure he doesn't get away. I'll be back." She spotted Justin enter the bar with a hesitant gait. "Sorry," she apologized. "I have to put out a fire on the casino floor, but the Chairman is going to keep you company until I can get back."

Entering the table games pit it became apparent why Ann had called. There were some situations only the casino manager could straighten out. In disputes with customers, it was her responsibility to make a final decision. She was where the buck stopped. She found Jenny Chin crying her eyes out at a three-card poker table.

Spying Caroline, she screamed, "I won the jackpot, and they are trying to cheat me out of my money."

The other players at the table bombarded her, a jumble of voices shouted. "It's all the dealer's fault." Players always liked to blame the dealer, but like all professionals dealers rarely made mistakes.

"We saw Jenny put her dollar in," one player said.

"Yeah, we did," another claimed. "The casino is trying to steal her money."

Security guards hovered in the background, ready to step in if the players became too hostile. The dealer, a woman named June, quivered like she was also on the verge of tears. She tried to talk to Jenny but got nowhere. "Luvvy, I am so sorry. I did remind you to bet the bonus. You said maybe next hand."

"I'll go check the tape." Caroline gave June the look, the signal to dummy up and deal. "Restart the game."

The progressive bet was a side bet that transformed a table game into a slot machine. If a player held an Ace, King, and Queen of diamonds, clubs, or hearts they won five hundred dollars. The Ace, King, and Queen of spades won the entire progressive jackpot which had grown to eighteen thousand dollars. The only problem was that the player had to bet the dollar every hand. Apparently, Jenny had skipped the one hand when she was dealt the magic cards.

Upstairs in surveillance Caroline studied the tape with Joanna. "I can clearly see that June asked her if she wanted to play the dollar." She pointed to the freeze frame display on the screen of June pointing to the slot, waiting for Jenny to drop her dollar down it before she locked the bets. Once a hand was locked, a light would glow red above the slot if the player made their progressive bet.

The video clearly showed Jenny raise her head, shake it no, then lay her head back on the table. The progressive light on her hand was not lit up, proof she hadn't played it.

"Once again, Jenny is falling asleep at the table." Caroline pushed her hands through her hair in exasperation. "Now, I have to go down and burst her bubble. I wish she had won the damn thing but she didn't so I can't pay her. Although if she did win it, we both know, she would just lose it again in a few hours. She's in the last stages of her gambling addiction, the one where she wants to lose all her money."

"Good luck," Joanna said as she rose. "This has been a long session for her. She was playing here when I came to work yesterday. That makes forty-eight hours straight. Sometimes I'm glad I get to hide in this room."

Back downstairs, Jenny had laid her head on the table and appeared to be asleep. The other players, having exhausted their outrage, now concentrated on playing their hands. Once again, the strangest things became normal in a casino.

Caroline nudged Jenny awake. "I'm sorry, you didn't play the Progressive. But you did win four hundred dollars from your pair plus bet, not too shabby. Let me comp you a room in the hotel, and when you get there order some room service. My treat, I won't count it against your points."

A bleary-eyed Jenny gazed up at Caroline. She probably believed she had played her dollar but had depleted all her energy. Defeated, she nodded her head. "Okay. Whatever."

Caroline led her up to a room in the hotel, ordered room service for her, waited for it to arrive, and then excused herself.

She hurried back to the Chop House before she had to deal with another emergency. An hour had passed, and she expected that Justin would have given up on her. She was excited to see him still drinking at the bar with John. She joined them. "Chairman Tovar, do you mind if I steal Justin from you? I'm really hungry." Her stomach growled to emphasize the statement.

As the waiter led them to a table, John and Brandon took their seats at a booth across and behind them. For herself, Caroline was glad she had a clear view of the two men in case something unexpected happened.

She loved the Chop House, the fancier of the Night Hawk's restaurants, serving over-priced steaks and seafood. Every casino needed an expensive restaurant, a place they could comp their players to. Unaware a sting was being played out right around them, patrons celebrated anniversaries, birthdays, and other special events. The dimmed lights in the room lent an air of intimacy. A place to exchange secrets, the perfect setting for a film noir. She slid into the plush leather booth.

They ordered their food, two cowboy rib eyes and a bottle of red wine. Ready to start her performance, Caroline picked up her cell phone. "I need to check back in with Ann."

Instead, she dialed Brandon's number and waited for his answering machine to pick up. "Everything okay in the pit?" she asked. Then she pushed a button that replaced the call screen with her screen saver. Justin thought she had hung up, but Brandon could hear every word of their conversation.

She placed her cell phone on the table. "Sorry, I have to keep my phone near me at all times. You never know when trouble will come calling, only that it will. But for now, you have my full attention. So…tell me why you enlisted in the Marines."

"I grew up on an apple farm in Missouri and joined the Marines after college, looking for excitement and travel." By this time, he was slurring his words. "Sometimes I think I got more excitement than I bargained for. I didn't even know we were at war with Syria." It sounded like he was saying *cereal* but she knew what he meant. "There I was, dodging bullets all the same. I like my job here at the base, handling the supplies, it's safe."

She baited the hook. "Ann says you're a computer expert."

"I try to keep my skills current. I use computers to keep track of my supplies, ma'am." The waiter arrived with steaks sizzling on hot plates. "This smells fantastic." Inebriated, his red cheeks glowed.

She took a bite of steak then laid down her fork. "I would like a new laptop to do my work at home. Can you suggest one for me to buy?"

The waiter topped up their glasses of wine. Feeling guilty, she plied Justin with alcohol. She liked the guy and hoped he was innocent. Either way she would find out soon. As they ate their dinner, she sipped her wine. He gulped his.

"Different computers are better at different things." Even drunk the subject animated him. For the next hour he advised her about the various features of different laptops. While he droned on about screen size, storage, and pixels, she feigned interest.

166

Right after they ordered desert, he paused his lecture to offer her a bargain. "I have the best model for you in my van, right here in the parking lot. I can sell it to you for three hundred dollars."

To keep up the pretense, her eyes went wide. "I've checked prices of computers in the stores. That's a great price for what I was looking at. How do you do it?"

"Let's say it fell off the back of a truck," he said.

"It's a deal. I think I have that much in my wallet. I always like to carry some emergency cash on me."

He picked up his cell phone and made a call, speaking in a foreign language.

After they had savored the last bites of their bananas Foster, Assam and Hassan appeared at the table. Assam carried a laptop. He handed it to Justin who passed it over the table to Caroline.

She ran a loving hand over the smooth surface. "I love it, it's perfect."

Justin grabbed her hand. "You sure are pretty, ma'am. I can come over to your house, program it for you, and teach you how to use it."

This was almost too easy. "That would be great, but I have to go back to work now. Give me your phone number; I'll call you when I have my next night off." She rose from her seat. "Do you need a ride home? The casino can get you a taxi."

"These guys will take me home." He pointed to his friend. "Hassan is my driver."

Hassan put his hands together pointing to the sky. "Praise Allah. We don't drink, we will get him home safely."

All of a sudden Justin stood and lunged at Caroline, going in for a kiss. Horrified, she ducked her head to avoid him. His arms swiped her wine glass which crashed to the floor, breaking into shards. Red wine splattered across her crème-colored suit. He slumped against the table. His friends rushed in to grab him before he hit the floor.

Amir steadied him. "We will take him home now. He must be overcome by your beauty."

Alerted by the commotion their waiter reappeared and said, "Don't worry, Ms. Popov, I will take care of this mess."

Her cell phone rang. John whispered on the other end, "Get the hell out of here, now!" Looking up, she noticed Brandon and him slip out of the Chop House.

"I have to apologize again," she said to Justin. "I'm so sorry, I really have to leave. They need me on the casino floor."

She stepped outside the restaurant and handed the computer to Brandon who was waiting for her. She returned to work disappointed at how fast her perfectly choreographed noir segued into slapstick.

At the end of the shift, as she filled out the nightly win/loss reports, she noticed, not for the first time, that the hold should have been larger. A triumphant looking John Tovar and General Brisson, both dressed in civvies stood in front of her. John closed the door to her office. They plopped down in seats in front of her desk.

John broke the silence. "I want you to know Joanna told me that she got everything on tape."

"I just wanted to thank you on behalf of the Marines. Here is a very small token of our appreciation." The general laid a Marine baseball cap on her desk. "After you gave Brandon the computer, we followed Justin home, careful to cut our lights when his van turned down a dirt road. His lives near the Big Rock outside of Landers." The name described it well, it was the largest free-standing boulder in the world, seven stories high. "The military police tracked the serial number on the computer to verify it was stolen from the base."

John interrupted him. "All of a sudden we were in the middle of a crime scene. With the help of the local police, they raided his house. After the arrests, they let us in. It looked like he was running the Base Exchange from there. In the front room we found laptops, computers, air conditioners, along with cigarettes and liquor. But he hid the high dollar stuff in the back rooms, automatic rifles, machine guns, pistols, and body armor. He thinks the military police were following him. He has no idea we played any part in his arrest."

The general jumped back in. "The MPs escorted Justin and his buddies back to the base for interrogation. After a friendly conversation, Assam and Hassan confessed that they fenced most of the stuff they stole through their contacts in Los Angeles, but the stuff in the back-rooms Justin sold to a militia group in Nevada. It's pretty scary to think militia groups are being supplied by some treasonous Marines. The size of the operation surprised me. I hate to imagine what damage could have been done if domestic terrorists had gotten hold of those weapons."

She smiled watching the two play macho men. Pumped on adrenaline, their chests puffed up as they spoke. It was a bittersweet moment because they all knew that the story of their exploits would never leave this room. There would be no medals or certificates of appreciation. The public could never find out how closely the casino worked with the government and law enforcement. That would not be good for business.

She fingered the pendant she wore around her neck. "My lucky charm is working. Everyone played their parts perfectly. John, I told you we could pull this off and I would never be in any harm."

"Don't forget old loudmouth," John protested. "I loosened Justin up for you."

"I only have one question." Caroline sipped on hot chocolate. "What is the title of our film noir?"

John smirked. "The answer is obvious, *Casino Queen*, in honor of our femme fatale."

Caroline blushed. "I didn't bring Justin down; he did it to himself. Overconfidence kills, the thief always thinks he's a little bit smarter than everybody else. Justin convinced himself the casino wanted his business so badly we would never report him."

The general stood up. "I have to get home now, I'm beat." He walked over to the door and glanced back at them. "BAMCIS."

Perplexed, Caroline asked, "What does that mean?"

"It means, begin the planning, arrange reconnaissance, make reconnaissance, complete the plan, issue the order, and supervise. Basically, it's Marine speak for a successfully completed mission."

John said, "I'll lead you out, general. We don't want anyone to see you."

"Just another day at the office," Caroline said as the two men disappeared into the night.

Chapter Twenty-One

Most of Being a Casino Manager is not Glitz and Glamour, Just Paperwork

On a sleepy Tuesday morning, Caroline decided to tackle the paperwork piled up on her desk. Since the casino business was basically a numbers game, after a couple hours, her eyesight blurred from studying all the columns of figures. The numbers appeared like elongated versions of themselves. Thick piles of paper covered her desk.

She sighed, overwhelmed by the stacks of revenue reports to review: food and beverage, the slot department, table games, and the hotel. Keeping track and making sense of all the money that passed through the casino was ultimately her responsibility as casino manager.

Reports arrived on her desk at the end of every shift, every day, every week, and every month of the year. All needed to be studied for patterns, what were the most profitable days, what was the drop, what was the hold? What games brought in the most revenue? Which tables were the most profitable? She studied the patterns of the red card holders. Were they coming to the casino regularly? If not, what could the casino do to entice them to come back? With twenty casinos within driving distance, competition for every dollar remained fierce. Revenue was the name of the game. Just like any corporation they answered to their shareholders, except at Native American casinos the stockholders were the tribes.

She rubbed her itching eyes and opened them, surprised to find Joanna standing in front of her, carrying papers in her hand. "You startled me." *John was right, Joanna was an outstanding tracker. I never heard her enter the room.*

With a flourish Joanna handed her a blue flyer decorated with a stencil of a crescent moon and a purple mountain in the background. The words *'Night Half Marathon at Joshua Tree'* in bold print sprawled across the page.

"What do you say, can we count you in?" Joanna asked. "It's great for local charities. The tribe donates one hundred dollars on behalf of each employee who runs. I am running for autism research."

Visions of sprinting through the giant rocks as the moon rose in the sky passed through her mind. "A night run does sound like fun. I used to be pretty talented at running back in the day."

"I bet you played basketball."

"Did my height give me away? Wrist injuries sidelined me, but I think my legs are still working. Training for this run would be great excuse for me to get out of this office. Sure, sign me up. Anything for the tribe."

Joanna motioned to the chair in front of Caroline's desk. "Can I chat with you?"

She pushed the papers to the side. "I'd love a break from work."

Joanna sat down and hesitated. "It's hard for me to

do this. I'm not wrong very often but I just want to apologize. I feel like I have been giving you a hard time since you got here. I know you are trying so hard to clean up this place, and I should be your biggest cheerleader. I don't know why but I resented you at first. Even though I could never take on the role of casino manager with all my responsibilities at home, I just wanted them to ask me."

Caroline sympathized with Joanna. "It's so nice to hear you say that. I need the support of longtime employees like you, especially tribal members." She wanted to get up from her desk and give Joanna a hug but she didn't know if it would be welcomed. Instead she offered a simple, "Thank you."

"Did you know that John broke the law to start this casino?"

Caroline had heard this story many times before, but she wanted to bond with Joanna, so she pretended she hadn't. "I'm fuzzy on the details. Tell me exactly what he did."

"Years ago when we first decided to open the casino in Palm Springs, we were exploring a partnership with a huge Vegas casino. They would take over the day-to-day operations for a cut of the profits. The Vegas casino was on board, but they met resistance from the other casinos in Vegas who were scared of the competition from California casinos. The state of Nevada put so much pressure on them that they pulled out of the arrangement. The tribe found themselves stuck with an empty building and truckloads of slot machines on order. John decided to have the slot machines delivered and installed in the middle of the night even though it was against the law." She imitated

John. "He always said, 'If they want to shut us down, they have to come through me.' "

Caroline crossed her arms and said, "That sounds like John, the tribe always comes first."

"We opened the casino the next day, and until Proposition Five, legalizing Native American casinos, was passed by the citizens of this great state, we operated every day terrified federal marshals would come in and shut us down. I feel so grateful to John because his decisions allowed me to raise my son and get him the help he needs. I'm sure you can understand how much it would destroy me to let John down. But let me go before things get too sticky in here. I'm not used to eating crow, although my ancestors probably did."

After her awkward attempt at a joke Joanna rose from her chair. Her cell phone buzzed, she dipped her head to read the message. "Do you mind if I leave early today? I have to pick my kid up from school, teacher conference time. Ahote is a bit hard to control, like his mother."

"Sure, but I need some advice from you before you go. If I am going to run this race, I need some new sporting gear. Can you recommend the best place to buy it?" Caroline wanted to keep the conversation going a little bit longer. She was beginning to understand why John thought Joanna was such a bad ass bitch.

She welcomed this half-marathon as the excuse to change her life. She promised herself that in spite of her busy schedule she would carve out time to make healthy meals and train every day. Enthused by her new resolutions, she wanted to start right now.

That evening, on her way home she drove to a

Yucca Valley sporting goods store where she purchased a sports bra, running shorts, a breathable T-shirt, and a pair of running shoes. She drove home elated to be able to spend money again.

Her body had suffered for too long from a diet of fast food, next stop was the grocery store for fresh produce and vegetables. Not only would she eat fresh food, she planned to prepare it herself. She would make the time to cook herself proper meals. Then she drove to the nearest big box store for a blender so she would be able to drink smoothies every morning after her run.

Before she crawled under the covers, she set the bedside alarm for five a.m. It seemed like only minutes had passed when the clock radio blasted music in her ear. Summoning up every ounce of her will, she fought against a body that desperately wanted to stay under the warm comforter. Instead, she dressed in her new sports attire and sat on the couch to lace up her new running shoes. The moment she stepped outside, the cold morning air caught her face. Starting down the hill guided by the moonlight, she took a second to watch the twinkling stars sprayed all over the purple desert sky. Then she ran.

Exhausted by the time she reached the entrance to the highway, she leaned against a sign to rest before she started the long run back. Shots rang out in the distance. She jumped. Shocked, she searched the area and noticed the sign she was leaning on advertised the entrance to the gun range. Her head calmed down when she realized the shots were coming from there.

Reality about the current condition of her body began to set in as she started running up the hill to go home. Halfway up she began to sputter, winded and tired, so tired. Her feet ached. Out of shape but determined, she slogged on, jogging and walking until she caught a glimpse of her cabin in the distance. Entering through the front door, she collapsed on the couch exhausted but also exhilarated. Running was the kick in the butt she needed. To become a part of the desert, a part of this community, she needed to venture outside of the perpetual night of the casino.

Before work she whipped up a berry and banana smoothie, poured it into a tall glass, carried it out on the porch, flopped on the rocking chair, and then proceeded to savor every well-earned drop, as the sun rose over the mountains.

Chapter Twenty-Two

A Dealer Must Always be on the Alert

Happy, Caroline cruised down the road in her sporty red convertible, with the top down and Keith Urban blasting out of the radio. The great expanse of the High Desert surrounded her, and a brilliant blue painted the horizon. Free of debt at last and feeling lucky to be on her way to a challenging job, she'd recently let herself believe life could be good. It wasn't just a slogan printed on a T-shirt.

If only Andrei still loved her, life would be complete. Her heart stung just a little bit, but she reminded herself, in life as in blackjack you can't play the last hand. That's in the past. You have to play the cards in front of you now.

Resolved to stay in the present, she maneuvered into her coveted parking space closest to the casino, reserved for the casino general manager. She picked up her purse and was about to open her car door when out of nowhere, Derrick of Donegal appeared, blocking her exit from the car by strategically placing his hands on either side of the door.

"Well, I finally have you to myself, Ms. Popov." A menacing grimace plastered across his face. "Can you tell me one thing, why did you fucking blackball me from being hired at every California casino? Firing me wasn't punishment enough for you?"

He leaned into the car window so close to her face that she could see every vein bulging out of his forehead and smell his breath, which reeked of cigarette smoke. "I believe that you got yourself blackballed. The last time I checked, extortion, oh excuse me, loans from employees to managers, were illegal." She was shaking inside but she must maintain her composure. "Now please get out of my way."

Jamar cycled up and stopped beside them. "Is this gentleman bothering you, Ms. Popov?"

Once again, she was thankful that security patrolled the parking lot to stop the crazies before they made their way in the front door.

Defeated, Derrick began to back away from the car. "I'm not through with you, bitch. You'll be seeing me again. After all, I do have a lot of time on my hands, thanks to you. Just to let you know, be on your guard because when you least expect it, I'll be there, and we'll finish this conversation."

She couldn't be having Derrick ruin her day every time she drove into the parking lot. "We won't be having this conversation here. You are permanently banned from the Night Hawk and any other property the Shotowa own."

"That's all right, I know where to find you."

At that moment Hector joined them. "Do you want me to take care of him, Ms. Popov?" He held up a pair of handcuffs. "I can cuff him." His wiry muscles tensed. He would relish making mincemeat of a poseur like Derrick.

Although she would love to sic security on Derrick, watch him crumble in Hector's arms, she decided a public beating in the parking lot wouldn't be a wise idea. "We'll let him go this time." Not in front of the customers, that's what back rooms were for. She stared Derrick right in the eye to make sure he understood. "But if you ever see him on this property again, beat the shit out of him."

As soon as she got to her desk, she called Brandon to ask for a restraining order against Derrick. "I don't know why but in all my years of dealing he is the only person I have ever been scared of. I can't get rid of him. Like a bill collector, he keeps showing up."

In a battle with the devil you had to pull out the big guns. He was already invading her dreams. She couldn't let him ruin her days. Sometimes she woke from the same nightmare where Derrick and all the people that she had conflicts with at the casino morphed into one face, screaming and cursing at her. Every time a black sedan passed by her cabin, her heart stopped. For the first time in her life, she faced real threats from people who might just be crazy enough to follow through. The police still hadn't found out who painted the billboard. Hopefully, having a restraining order against Derrick would allow her to sleep at night.

Caroline's day flew by quickly. Deanna called first. "There is a new player who owns a wind farm. She wants to establish a credit limit of $50,000. Can you okay it?"

Next, she met with the bar manager. "I am interviewing for a new bartender, replacing the last one who gave away more liquor than he sold. I would like you to meet her, get your approval."

Ann approached her in the cafeteria. "I want to make Ling employee of the month to reward her for the way she handled the game when chaos broke out all around her."

Every hour she swanned the gaming floor, taking a mental count of the play. At odd times she found herself replaying the conversation with Derrick while trying to study the endless reports that crossed her desk and ate up huge chunks of her time. No matter how she scheduled her day, she was always distracted because each day was filled with problems that needed to be fixed, now! The incident with Derrick receded farther and farther into the back of her mind, to a place reserved for unpleasant memories.

Ten hours after Derrick interrupted her day, she got back into her car. Spooked when she noticed a black sedan behind her following a little too closely, her legs began to shake. Swerving into the closest driveway, a fast-food restaurant, she began breathing much easier after the sedan continued on the road. Guess I'm having chicken for dinner. She headed for the drive-through.

There was a ritual to her meals, even the takeout ones. She put her food on the counter of her kitchen, opened the cabinet, lifted out the good china, and carefully set herself a place at the table. Before she ate, she performed one last ritual, transferring her chicken from the bags to the heavy blue and white porcelain plates. Andrei grew up in Russia, which was not a throw-away culture. He would never eat off of a paper plate and convinced her that food eaten off of good china always tasted better. He believed that it was the little things that transformed food into a meal.

After dinner she poured herself a glass of wine, carried it out to the porch, positioned herself on the rocking chair, picked up her cell phone, and dialed her friend Mindy Oxendine. She was thrilled to have a friend she could call, someone who could relate to her. They shared the same struggle, trying to make their way in a world dominated by male testosterone. Tonight, like every night, they gossiped about casinos and the Bureau of Indian Affairs.

There was also a ritual to the bath. After she hung up the phone, she lay herself down in the bathtub and twisted on the tap. Her body began to relax as hot water slowly enveloped her legs and steam rose all around her. When the water level rose halfway up the tub, she squirted some bath oil under the faucet, and the fragrant liquid beaded up on her skin. She believed that there was no better way to be in the moment than immersed in a tub. Filling up the tub was part of the ritual, as inch by inch of her body was covered with water. Whenever she tried meditation unwanted thoughts dominated her mind, but when warm water surrounded her body, she achieved a peaceful state of bliss.

The cell phone rang, but she let it go to voicemail. No cell phones were allowed in the bathroom. Work would just have to wait. Drowsy after her bath, she crawled into bed and picked up her current novel, one of her preferred thrillers. On her days off she still binge-watched television series about rotten men, con artists who cheated women out of their life savings, bigamists that claimed they worked for the CIA, and serial killers who searched for lonely women to kill. And now with streaming services she had a whole world of international misery to watch.

After a few pages, her book slipped from her hands to the floor. From the edge of sleep a picture of Derrick rocking on her porch flashed behind her eyelids. His evil face replaced the face of the villain in her novel, startling her back to the incident from this morning, which seemed like a bad dream, that happened a long time ago in a faraway place.

Chapter Twenty-Three

Casino Security Guards Come to Work Every Day Hoping for a Confrontation

Caroline detected a note of panic in John's voice. "I just read yesterday's incident report. You didn't tell me Derrick threatened you in the parking lot. Please humor me and stay in the hotel for the next few weeks until we know that you are safe."

"I will do no such thing. I am training for the half-marathon. Besides, you don't really take any of those threats seriously, do you?"

She tried to convey confidence even though the image of Derrick haunted her dreams. John must not find out that if she noticed a black sedan behind her on the highway, she lost sensation in her legs and would have trouble pressing her foot to the gas pedal. It was important that John didn't doubt that she could handle this job and all the crap that came with it. Most of the time she operated like an athlete in training. The rush of adrenaline mixed with fear pumped her up.

She wouldn't quit even if this job killed her. "With you, Brandon, and the entire Shotowa tribal police force protecting me, what could go wrong?"

"Five years ago I would have said nothing, but these days the world is such a crazy place. Have you already forgotten that just last month two gang members got shot in a gunfight in front of the Palm Oasis? I shudder to think about what would have happened to a bystander if they had gotten in their way. They could have been killed. Let's say we compromise. I am buying you a gun and I am going to teach you to shoot. I am also making sure that the police monitor your cabin."

"Fine, there is a gun range at the bottom of my road. I run past it every morning. I've always been a bit curious about what happens there. Now that this is settled, let me get back to work, at least for the remaining time I have left on this Earth."

"Don't even joke about that. I have lost way too many people. Gun violence isn't funny. I'll meet you at six." And then the conversation shifted to the mundane matters involved in running a casino.

She met John at the range, a vast outdoor space which backed into a mountain. The young clerk dressed in a polo shirt sporting the company logo, very preppy, then she noticed his holster packed with a pistol. Her hands began to shake as she leaned over the counter hesitating to pick up the pistol that she would use for target practice that day, a small black gun with a long slide. It terrified her to think that if she made a wrong move, this gun could end a life, possibly her own. She willed away the panic attack building in her chest.

The clerk, Everett, must have noticed her discomfort. "Don't be nervous. I will show you how to handle this pistol. By the time you leave here, you'll be shooting like a pro. I make sure no one gets hurt on my watch." He picked up the gun demonstrating as he talked. "Always point the gun straight ahead, especially when you are loading the bullets." Using his pistol, he unloaded the magazine, pushing the rounds out one by one. "The gun will hold seventeen full metal jackets, then you reload the magazine and you're good to go." Next there were lessons on cocking the gun and shooting.

Instead of calming her down, the training was making her even more anxious, especially when she put on her goggles and ear defenders.

Everett led them outside to a series of wooden stalls all set in a row. The bleakness of the scenery, devoid of anything but rocks and dirt containing wide open spaces perfect for letting bullets fly. They placed their guns on a shelf, a box of ammunition lying between them. Caroline's hands shook so hard that John loaded the bullets for her. "I will do this for you now, but then you will have to learn to handle this on your own."

He placed the loaded gun in her hand and stood next to her as she pointed the barrel at the target, a paper cutout of a menacing cartoon villain pointing a gun at her—a duel in the desert. Gingerly she pulled the trigger. Nothing happened. Then using all the strength her fingers could muster, gave it another go. A loud boom echoed against the mountain, and an acrid odor infused the air. She jumped back startled by the force of the gun.

The shell casing popped out of the chamber and hit her eyes, covered with safety goggles. "Now I know why I am wearing these goggles. That gun has quite a kick." Whenever the sound of gunfire reverberated across the range, a chill ran through her.

After many tries, she finally learned how to load the gun, but the chamber kept jamming after she fired.

With each shot a visceral terror grew inside her. She kept picturing herself pumping bullets into Derrick while she listened to him plead for mercy. Relieved when she used up her box of ammunition, she realized that she would never feel comfortable shooting a gun.

John pulled in the target, unclipped it and examined the paper cutout riddled with bullet holes. "Well, you shot him all right, but all the bullets landed in the groin area."

"That's where I was aiming. I wanted to maim the guy, not kill him."

"Now I am going to buy you a pistol for your purse. I hear guns are the must have accessory this season."

"Thanks, but no thanks. I'm glad I learned how to shoot a gun, and now I am certain that I never want to shoot another one. A gun in your hand is way scarier than a gun on a movie screen. I would probably kill myself or be killed before I would ever manage to get the damn thing loaded. But you can buy me some pepper spray. That I might use." She picked up a small canister on the counter. "Let's get rid of these guns. They are giving me the creeps. What do you say? Let me buy you a drink?"

Situated on the only highway in the High Desert near the entrance to Joshua Tree National Park, there was a special bar, the kind that you hoped to find in cowboy country but weren't sure if a place like that really existed except in the movies. The national park attracted visitors from all over the world, and eventually most of them made their way there, certain they had discovered cowboy nirvana. Throw in some day hikers and locals, and by afternoon the place was packed with a diverse group of people with one goal in mind, they all knew how to party.

The restaurant served the usual bar fare, but the food wasn't the draw here. It was the friendly vibe. From the outside, the weathered wooden building looked like an old Western saloon, heavy on the wood: wooden bar, wooden tables, wooden walls, and wooden floors. The heavenly smell of sizzling burgers and frying onion rings assaulted their noses as they walked in the door, scoring the last two stools at the long bar.

After the waitress set their drinks down on the bar, Caroline picked up the menu laid on the counter. "Tonight grease is good. How boring, you ordered your usual gin and tonic. You're missing out. These margaritas are great." Caroline gasped as she sipped her frozen drink causing a *brain freeze.*

"I'm a man of many habits. Be glad that keeping my employees safe is one of them."

"I always believed Andrei would keep me safe. I wish he were here." Caroline stopped, hoping that she hadn't revealed too much.

"Please repeat that. I was under the impression that you kicked him to the curb. I don't mean to pry, but yeah, I really do."

She noticed that for the first time in a while John's full attention was directed at her. "What the heck, they say confession is good for the soul. No, I never stopped missing Andrei, but one day I had to admit he wasn't coming back. I'll admit I screwed up. Over the years I have realized that leaving him was the worst mistake I ever made. I let him down. If only I could have a do over."

"I thought he deserted you. He's the one who

stayed in Russia."

"He wanted me to stay, too. I snuck out in the middle of the night and boarded the ship. When he confessed that we had lost everything, I couldn't handle it. We promised each other that we would always be there for richer and poorer, and the first time we were poorer, I ran away." She picked at the peanuts sitting in a dish in front of her, trying to avoid John's eyes. "From the day I met him, what won me over was his confidence, his complete conviction about everything he did. Once he lost his confidence, I lost mine. He wasn't the only one who lost his way. I did too."

"But then you would be living in Russia. Is that what you are trying to say?"

"I'm not sure. I should have stayed for a while, long enough to convince him to come home with me. My pride let me lose the only person who really truly loved me in a way that I didn't believe possible. My life was too sensible and boring before I met Andrei. He brought color into my life. I am such a coward."

He brushed a stray hair off her face. "You could try to win him back. It might not be too late."

"It really is. Don't think less of me, but I have to tell you the worst thing I ever did." She cast her eyes toward the floor. "Shortly after I started working at the casino, I called him in Russia and told him I slept with someone else. I made a mistake, told a lie, because I wanted to put a nail in our coffin. After I began to work for you, his distraught mother called me. She believed that he was on the verge of a breakdown and that I should either return to Russia or let him go. She loved him so much. I took her words to my broken heart. We were so deep in a hole. We owed the IRS so much money, realistically I calculated it would take years to climb out of debt, and I was right. I wanted to make sure that he would never call me again because talking to me was tearing him apart. My crazy plan, once I paid the debt, would be to get in touch with him and confess, but it took so many more years than I imagined. Now at this late date, I'm pretty sure even if he doesn't love anyone else, he's finished with me."

"Adultery is a pretty big nail." He took her hand in his. "I'll protect you, Caroline."

She studied his face filled with concern for his friend. She could understand why women fell madly in love with him, he made you feel like the most important person in the world. He smiled his inscrutable smile. "Let me be clear, I won't sleep with you, and I certainly won't marry you, but I will protect you." After a moment of uncomfortable silence, they both laughed and things between them returned to normal.

She grimaced. "Don't worry, I couldn't marry you anyway because I'm still married."

John seemed surprised. "I always wondered why you went by the name Popov. It's been a really long time."

"Didn't see any need to get a divorce. I figured if Andrei wanted one, he could find me. I've never loved anyone but Andrei, always only him."

"I know this is really awkward, but does that mean that you haven't, how shall I put this, done the deed with anyone else all these years?"

Her face turned the color of beets while she sucked on the dregs of her drink. "I've done it, as you so delicately put it, with two people. The first time was with that charming dealer from Indio Springs, Rick. He reminded me of a Greek god and I was pretty sure that he wasn't dying to get into a serious relationship. Friends with benefits worked for a while. I just needed to prove to myself that everything still worked.

"The second person was a bit of a fluke. A player at my game entered a movie into the film festival in Palm Springs. He came from New Zealand. They don't call it America's largest international film festival for nothing. The producers gave a talk to the audience, and at the end they invited us over to Melvyn's for a drink."

John cocked his head toward her and grinned.

"Don't stare at me that way. What can I say, I'm a sucker for an accent, except for Derrick's."

"Have you ever searched for Andrei on social media?"

"No. And reaching out to him terrifies me, kind of like shooting a gun. I know this sounds horrible, but it's true, I'm scared I might find him happy without me."

****

Painful memories of Andrei flooded her mind that night. Finally, she drifted into a disturbed sleep until the early morning when the alarm jolted her awake. Determined not to let fear get the best of her, she laced up her running shoes, opened the front door, hit the pavement, and started all over again, but as a precaution she carried her cell phone and pepper spray.

Dragging herself up the hill to her cabin after her run, she was surprised to find Brandon up a ladder on her porch, his well-toned butt on display. Well, she reasoned, she could appreciate the view. She just couldn't touch.

John, rocking away in her favorite chair, supervised. "I told you I would protect you. I am introducing a new policy. I plan to install surveillance cameras at the homes of our senior managers. This way you can constantly monitor your surroundings, and if you notice anything unusual, don't hesitate, call Brandon."

Caroline should be annoyed, but instead relief flooded through her. "You should have consulted me first, but I suppose I wouldn't have stopped you. To be honest, I guess that's not too weird—most homes have security systems."

Looking down from his ladder Brandon spoke. "Sorry, Ms. Popov, I blame myself for not acting sooner. I want you and John to be able to sleep at night. Give us a few minutes and I will show you how to use the equipment."

"Thank you. What can I make you guys for breakfast? I make a pretty tasty smoothie. I'm starving."

That evening she didn't turn on the television. Instead, watching the cars passing on the road became her favorite show of the week.

Chapter Twenty-Four

Sometimes a Manager Can Learn More from Listening Than Talking

One gray morning, a windstorm blew through the desert. Sand blasted Caroline as she fought against the wind stinging her eyes, making her way to the entrance of the Night Hawk.

A voice behind her competed with the wind. "Come, check out my wheels, Ms. Popov. Let me show you under the hood." Hector stood beside a shiny new car. He swaggered around to the front and raised the hood, glancing around the lot, making sure he was noticed.

Throughout the years, Caroline grew quite accustomed to tribal members turning up in new wheels, trying to one up each other. Even though she desperately wanted to get out of the wind, if she didn't stop to compliment his car it would be a blow to his ego. "I'm confused, there's nothing there, where is the engine?"

"Under the floor in the back, a battery pack. That is the beauty of an electric car," he bragged. "The guy who invented this car is going to travel to Mars."

Feigning interest, she listened politely as he recited all the bells and whistles, his enthusiasm lost on her. The only thing she needed from an automobile was a smooth ride on the bumpy desert roads. For the rest of the day whenever she made her rounds around the casino, everyone was talking about Hector's swishy new ride.

For security reasons she preferred to dispose of her own documents, plus it was a great excuse to escape the office. She made her way down the back stairs to the industrial strength paper shredder, carrying a stack of reports in her hands. The shredder shared a hallway with the employee cage. Fascinated by the strength of the shredder, she watched its teeth gobble up a stack of papers in one go.

While she fed papers into the machine, her front facing the wall, two security guards hoisted heavy glass boxes filled with empty racks onto the counter of the employee cash desk. Unaware of her presence, they shot the breeze as they waited for the cashiers to fill their racks with chips to replace the chips that players won at the tables. Praying they wouldn't notice her, she overheard them debating the pros and cons of luxury cars that they would never be able to afford.

"Give me a sports car any day. You can't beat an American classic."

"I don't know, an off roader is more practical. That baby will take you so far in the wilderness, no one will ever find you."

"But I have to admit that model S Hector bought is a real beauty. The car is sleek, electric, and it connects to the Internet. I wish I was a Shotowa."

He sounded envious. Who wouldn't be? Even Caroline was slightly jealous of the generous stipend the tribe shelled out to its members every month.

The other security guard shook his head. "Nah,

Hector isn't a Shotowa. He comes from a tribe near Yuma. I forget their name, but they don't have a casino. I know because Hector complains all the time, says he was born into the wrong tribe, how only a few hundred miles makes all the difference in the world."

Wistfully, shaking his head, his co-worker replied, "We were all born into the wrong tribe. I wish they would hurry up with this fill."

"Why? Waiting is kind of like a break. Enjoy it. You're on the clock and all you have to do is stand here."

Later that afternoon she perused Hector's personnel file. She spread it out on her desk, congratulating herself on her superior snooping skills. She gleaned so much valuable information eavesdropping on conversations around her. She vowed to become a private detective in her next life.

Could Hector be stealing? It would be really stupid to drive a $100,000 car to a job where you made under $60,000 if you were stealing from your employer, but maybe it was a double bluff. The file praised his eclectic skills. His duties included lead security on the drop and maintaining the drop boxes. The combination of those two duties set off warning bells in her mind.

Reluctantly she added Hector to the mental list in her head of all the employees she was keeping an eye on, potential thieves lurked everywhere. Yesterday Ling accidentally paid a push and Caroline watched her for half an hour to make sure she wasn't cheating. Every time a dealer made a mistake on a payout or paid a push, she tried to give them the benefit of the doubt but later questioned her decision.

A fine line existed between mistakes and stealing,

but she agreed with Joanna. *"When you work in the money store, everyone starts to believe it's their money."*

It was her job to be extra vigilant not paranoid, but it was hard to tell when the lines crossed. Working as a dealer, she had witnessed people being fired for stealing who she would have sworn would never steal, like Abigail. She needed to proceed slowly. She didn't want to ruin Hector's life over a hunch.

At that moment her cell phone rang. Mindy's name and smiling face flashed across the screen. Caroline relaxed, happy to have someone convince her that she wasn't a paranoid mess, or maybe that she was.

Chapter Twenty-Five

Social Media Makes the Big World a Small Place

Stopping for a break in the employee lounge, lost in thought, Caroline spent this special day conjuring up all the regrets and sadness of the past. Today would have been her anniversary. Well, technically it still was, but without Andrei there, the day took on a special kind of sadness. Her life reminded her of the French story *The Necklace* written by Guy de Maupassant. When she read that story in school, she wondered how people could be so stupid to let pride ruin their life. Sadly, an older, wiser Caroline understood. At least Monsieur stuck by Mathilde as they worked off their debt. He hadn't run home to Russia.

Caroline worked all of these years to pay off a debt, ending up with nothing. Well, almost nothing. She touched her lucky charm necklace. The weight of it against her chest calmed her. Trying not to slip into despair, she sipped her hot chocolate. Nothing could cheer her up, but hot cocoa never hurt. She always preferred the sweetness of cocoa and sugar to the bitterness of coffee.

Her eyes scanned the break room, searching for someone she could talk to, but everyone was playing on their cell phones. Checking her own cell phone, she noticed the latest text from her biggest fan and decided he must be a financial advisor.

—We have to meet soon and plan a brilliant future together!—

The Internet had taken over, swallowed up conversation, no one spoke to each other anymore they just studied their screens as if they held the meaning of life. No wonder the casino seized the opportunity to exploit the World Wide Web. The marketing department employed people to take advantage of everything social media offered. Posting on the Internet proved to be a relatively cheap form of advertising with the ability to reach millions of people all over the world. Marketing set up accounts showcasing fun festive pictures of casino winners. They enticed players with tweets advertising special room rates, and on their official website customers left reviews, complaints, and questions about the casino.

A very glamorous photo of Caroline was plastered across all of the accounts. A few times names and faces from her past would appear hoping to rekindle a relationship, usually people she could only vaguely recall. As the face of the Night Hawk, she was always happy to reply with a personal message.

She took pride in her position and her title. Growing up she considered herself quite ordinary. Instead of giving her confidence, her height made her even more anxious to fit in with the crowd. If she could avoid it, she never spoke out in class or ran for student council. She would have rather died than try out to be a cheerleader. Joining the basketball team offered her a refuge. It meant she could be in the company of the other tall girls in school. Now after years in the casino business, she had loosened up, learned how to converse with anyone, movie stars, the local cops, her customers, and most importantly her employees. She had also developed a toughness that helped her manage hundreds of employees. Life had dealt her some heavy blows, but it also taught her that she didn't need anyone to take care of her. She was quite capable of taking care of herself.

Teresa from marketing walked toward her, tablet in hand. "I have another blast from the past for you. Do you mind if I join you?" She didn't wait for an answer as she plopped down into the seat across from Caroline. She passed her tablet across the table. "Do you remember someone called Erica Evergreen? She says she attended Long Beach State with you."

"Erica, the ultimate blast from the past. All I can remember is the terrible fight we got into. She was furious the last time I saw her." Caroline studied the profile picture of her friend. Her face older but just as alluring. "I can't believe this. Thank you."

"She didn't post on the casino page but instead sent you a direct message. She included her phone number." Teresa handed her a yellow post-it with a ten digit number sprawled across the front.

Shocked, surprised, and ecstatic, Caroline stood up and hugged Teresa. "This has really made my day." To make it through the present, sometimes you just have to face the past. "She was my best friend for years. I can't wait to talk to her."

Making her rounds around the casino, Caroline tried to tamp down her excitement, but couldn't contain it. She really wanted to call Erica. Entering her office she closed the door too quickly, accidentally slamming it, too nervous to sit. She hadn't been this excited since she met Mindy. Her voice shaking, Caroline asked her phone to dial Erica's number.

After a few tense seconds a phone rang, and then a familiar voice was speaking to her. "Hello."

Immediately Caroline burst into tears. "Erica, I can't believe I am really speaking to you. You don't know how often I have wondered about you throughout the years."

Erica's voice instantly transported her back to a simpler time, and who doesn't want to go there? "Me, too. I have been following you for a while, but I finally worked up the courage to message, next week I will be attending a mindfulness seminar at an institute near you. The one with the strange name. I hoped we could catch up while I am there."

"The building designed by Frank Lloyd Wright's son? I pass by there all the time. I always wondered what mental physics meant. You have to stay with me. You're right, we need to catch up." An invitation offered and accepted officially ended the very long feud between Caroline and Erica.

The next Friday night when Caroline pulled into her driveway, she noticed Erica's car already there and parked behind it. Carrying bags overflowing with groceries up the stairs, she found Erica happily rocking on the front porch.

"Sorry I'm late," she called up to her. "Putting out fires at the casino. I may be late, but I come bearing gifts of wine, cheese, and chocolate, our favorite foods. Come help me unload the car."

"I love your red car. Real swishy." Erica took a bag from the trunk.

"We bought it when we moved to Palm Springs.

Andrei loved everything American. He loved this convertible, the most American thing he could drive." Dammit, why did I mention Andrei? Erica hates him. They continued their conversation as they carried the bags inside.

"Are you two still together?" Erica asked in a casual way which made Caroline suspect that she already knew the answer.

"No, we broke up a while ago, well many years ago at this point. He lives in St. Petersburg now. What about you?" Caroline decided to change the subject to distract Erica. "I see you went blonde. We really could be sisters now."

"I always wondered if blondes really did have more fun, but it took me years to realize that I could just dye my hair. I believed you were the most confident and self-possessed person I knew and convinced myself it was because you were blonde. I have to confess, the way you and Andrei formed a bond, became a team, consumed me with jealousy. I was jealous because you were living the romance we both wanted. I am sincerely sorry you broke up. Even I want to believe love can last."

"You thought I was confident? Everything I knew about life I learned from the romance novels we read in college when we should have been studying. Those books taught me that men only loved people they could save. I wasn't an alcoholic, didn't suffer from any childhood traumas, and I didn't pop pills. I was convinced I was the most boring person on Earth, especially next to my glamorous best friend, a reality tv star. I wasn't even a shopaholic." She opened the front door, speaking wistfully. "Then I met Andrei, who liked my predictability. His approval blew me away. But you were right about one thing, all the time we spent together was like a fairytale. I imagined myself a character in an animated film. Lines became clearer and colors were brighter. After all, we were drawn together in Southern California. But that was another life."

"What about now? You must have met some rich men in Palm Springs."

"Rich men," she said and shuddered. "They are the worst. Working at the casino has convinced me I never want to date a rich man. In romance novels rich men are kind, charming, patient, and handsome. In real life rich men are petty, abrasive, demanding, and for the most part ugly."

The sound of Erica's laugh felt like a balm. "What are the women who date them like? I want to be one."

"Demanding. They don't care what their men act like. They're just in it for the money. But they better get air-tight prenups because those guys aren't giving up anything that easily except at the gambling tables. My biggest regret, all the time Andrei and I wasted trying to get rich. I wish we had just lived in the moment. Did your conference teach you how to do that?"

Standing at the kitchen counter Caroline and Erica took a few seconds to stare at each other. For the first few minutes the conversation remained awkward but then they jumped back into the flow. All the years apart seemed to melt away.

Erica pulled up a picture on her cell phone. "This is my son, Julian. He's gorgeous." Her eyes shone. "His father spotted me on my reality dating show and messaged me, a bit of a fame whore. Eventually he left me for a newer younger model, a finalist on *America's*

Next Best Thing. Can't make this stuff up. Even though the marriage didn't last long, I have Julian, so I did get something from the show. He's staying with his father this weekend. As he gets older, I am scared I will lose him to his dad. Guy things, you know, but fortunately I am a better basketball player."

Across the desert sky a faraway storm brewing in the distance blasted brilliant white flashes of light followed by the booming sound of thunder. While the night progressed and the storm creeped closer, bottles of wine emptied, and revelations deepened. The two women lamented the sins of the past but decided to focus on the future.

"Erica, try out my invention, break off a block of chocolate, put a piece of cheese over it, and then bite. I call it choc and cheese." They each broke off some chocolate and topped it with cheese and bit. Sublime pleasure crossed over their faces. "Now, wash it down with some wine."

"I'm proud of us, I have taken over my parents' real estate agency, and you are the manager of a casino, a whole casino. A toast to us." Erica held up her wine glass. "Screw mindfulness. I need a few more weekends with old friends." They stared at each other like people who suddenly realized that they lived in a friendship desert. To celebrate they clinked their glasses together, and then sat in silence, listening to drops of rain hit the roof.

"I just realized you don't talk like a Valley girl anymore."

"You mean, I don't like, use the word, like, all the time, even though it adds no meaning to a sentence? When I watched myself on television I was appalled!

So, I took a course on elocution to learn to sound like a *LAADDY*," she drawled, carefully emphasizing each vowel.

Caroline laughed. "You know rain in the desert feeds the wildflowers, a good omen. If we're lucky we will wake up to a hill full of blooms."

The next morning Erica popped her head into a hungover Caroline's room. "Do you have any pills for a headache? I feel one coming on, and I want to nip it in the bud."

"Sorry I'm out, but I can go out and get some for you. My head is throbbing too. I think we could both use some help."

"No, you relax, I'll go. I could use the fresh air. I'll go to the drugstore I passed on the way here. Only your car is blocking me in."

"Here, take mine. The keys are in my purse, just take it with you. There's some cash in the wallet to pay for the pills, my treat. It's hanging on a hook in the kitchen."

"Sure. I always wanted to drive a convertible."

"Push the button on the far left of the dash to put the top down. If you have a problem the manual is in the glovebox." Caroline pulled the covers over her head. "Wake me when you get back."

After Erica left, Caroline drifted back to sleep, reviewing her plans for the perfect High Desert day. She wanted Erica to like the area so she would visit again. Caroline approved of the new grown-up Erica who appeared more subdued. After breakfast at the taco place, they would hike in Joshua Tree, and later go for happy hour at a bar where the waitresses dressed like saloon girls. A few hours later, unaware of the time,

Caroline woke to a knock on the door.

Expecting Erica, she was surprised to see two young policemen through the window, looking more like graduates from the local high school, not the training academy. Hesitantly, she opened the door. Shiny badges occupied a prominent space on their shirts.

They stared at her, perplexed. "Do you know Caroline Popov?"

"Yes. That's me." She hoped they hadn't found any more billboards wishing her dead, but maybe they found out who painted it. "How can I help you?"

"Do you know where your car is?" the shorter one inquired.

Her heart started pounding. "My friend borrowed it. Has something happened?"

"The driver of the car, your friend, I presume, was shot on the highway about three miles from here. She has been taken to the hospital."

"Oh my God! Whoever hurt her must have mistaken Erica for me!"

The other officer asked, "What would make you say that? Do you have any enemies?"

"Enemies? I'm the casino manager at the Night Hawk. Some days I think I have only enemies. Please tell me, is she okay?" Caroline pleaded. "She has to be okay!"

"We can't give out medical information, ma'am, but we can drive you to the hospital. After you leave the hospital, you'll have to come to the station for questioning."

Suddenly she realized she was in her night shirt. "I'll get dressed quickly."

On the way out the front door Caroline spotted Erica's satchel purse sitting on the coffee table. She picked it up and slung it across her shoulder.

A confused Caroline remained silent on the short tense drive to the medical center in Joshua Tree, the smallest hospital Caroline ever visited. When she came through the front door, she spied John waiting in the emergency room.

He jumped out of his chair as if he had seen a ghost. "I got a call about a gunshot on the highway because the car had a Shotowa employee parking permit, yours. They also found your gaming license in the car. I was sure whoever painted that billboard hurt you. But here you are." He pointed to the doors marked, *Medical Personnel Only.* "If you are here, who is lying in there?"

"My friend. I don't know how badly hurt she is. Does anyone have any information?"

She marched to the check-in window with John trailing behind her. The young African American nurse sat at a desk protected from the public by a wall of glass. "Do you have any information on my friend? They admitted her about an hour ago?"

"I'm sorry. I am not allowed to give out information about our patients without authorization." The nurse spoke in an official tone tinged with sympathy.

The smattering of people in the emergency waiting room began to take an interest in the conversation. Caroline read the nurse's nametag. "Kendra, there really isn't a Caroline Popov in there. I'm Caroline Popov. The person who got shot is my friend Erica Evergreen. She was driving my car." With her mind operating on panic mode, her speech rambled, jumping from one topic to another with little rhyme or reason. "People say we look alike. We don't really, but from a distance she resembles me. Please, she has to be okay. Is she okay?" She searched through Erica's purse finally producing her identification. She handed it to the nurse.

At that point the young officer interrupted them. "She's telling the truth."

John approached the desk. "Hello, my name is John Tovar, and I'm the Shotowa tribal chairman. I can vouch for the lady, she is my employee."

"I need to call the hospital administrator." She stepped away from her desk to make a phone call. When she returned, she turned to the group anxiously waiting in front of her.

"I've spoken to my boss." The nurse studied Erica's identification. "Can you find her insurance card?"

Caroline pulled out a card from Erica's wallet and handed it to the nurse. "Please, can we find out how she is doing?" Now that you know you'll get your money.

"We believe the patient was hit by a bullet while driving the car. Once the neurosurgeon arrives here from Palm Springs, she will be operated on. We called in a specialist because the bullet is in a precarious place, lodged into the back of her neck very close to the spine. You can wait here. Do you have the number of her husband or parents?"

At those words Caroline began to fall apart. "Get your act together," John demanded. "We have to contact her family. For that, you need to at least sound in control."

Caroline pulled out her cell phone and robotically searched for Erica's parents' information. Fortunately their real estate agency listed a phone number. "How can I tell Erica's parents that I might have gotten their daughter killed because of a mistaken identity? I let her visit me, stay in my home, even though I have been frightened for months. I didn't want you to think I was weak, so I acted tough."

He patted her shoulder. "I don't know, but you will find a way."

With fingers shaking and a tremor in her voice, Caroline made the hard call.

By the time Erica's parents arrived in Joshua Tree from Orange County, their daughter was lying in the operating room having a bullet removed. Caroline prepared herself for their anger, but instead they embraced her. Erica's mother always dressed immaculately, but today she arrived wearing jeans, her face makeup free. Her father appeared sans toupee. "We jumped in the car the minute you called. Please, tell us she is okay." They searched Caroline's face for reassurance.

John took over and held Erica's mother's hand. "Your daughter will be fine. I insist that you and your husband be my guest at the Night Hawk while you wait for your daughter to recover. I also promise you we will get to the bottom of this. We will find out who shot her." The soothing sound of his voice performed its magic, they calmed down. "Excuse me, I'll be back soon."

Erica's mother greeted Caroline through tear-stained eyes. "I regret we lost you. You were like another daughter to us. I was so glad when Erica told me she was coming to visit you. I am sorry we didn't keep in touch."

"I understand. She was your real daughter. I would have reacted the same way. Sometimes we all have to make hard choices."

Happy memories of Christmases, where there was always a present for her under the tree, seemed surreal as they waited for word of Erica's fate. Caroline wondered what their reaction would be if they knew who that bullet had been intended for.

She filled Erica's parents in on her diagnosis. Fortunately, a moment later, John returned, carrying sandwiches and coffee from a sandwich shop down the road. It was as if he had a sixth sense of what was needed in every situation. Starved, they devoured the food.

They squirmed as they waited in uncomfortable metal chairs in the waiting room. Many hours filled with strained conversation and long periods of silence passed before the surgeon, who identified himself as Dr. Nathanson, came out into the emergency waiting room dressed in his scrubs. Stray spiky gray hairs, escaped from under his headband. He appeared weary, his red eyes deeply etched with dark circles, a wan smile on his face. "I come bearing excellent news. We have successfully extracted the bullet. It came out clean, no damage. Now we just have to cross our fingers and hope for a full recovery. She will stay in intensive care tonight. You can see her in the morning."

Night had fallen on the desert by the time they walked outside. "Let's all go get some sleep."

As John led everyone to the parking lot, he gave the Evergreens directions to the casino. After they left, a depleted Caroline climbed into John's car for the drive home. "I am supposed to talk to the police. My car, I have to get my car. They towed it to Orenda & Sons Towing. They say it runs but was damaged running into a ditch when Erica got shot. I can't believe this is my new reality. My brain hurts but all that matters is that Erica doesn't die."

"But that doesn't mean you won't stress. We both know you were the target. I will call the station. Then I'll get your car picked up and take it to the body shop. Why don't we invite the officers over to your house?"

She yawned wide enough, long enough, to cause cracking sounds in her jaw. "Could you really make that happen? I am exhausted."

"It's great to be a big fish in a small sea. The tribe donates so much money to the police I am sure they'll be glad to come over if I ask them to. I am going to stay with you tonight, and tomorrow we will figure out the best way to protect you. For the time being I'll assign Brandon to be your bodyguard, someone you know and trust."

"I'm too tired to argue. Anyway, I could use the company. I'll never dismiss your warnings again." She showed him the guest room. "Give me a minute to tidy up, Erica slept here last night."

It took every bit of Caroline's energy for her leaden arms to strip the sheets Erica slept in. She just wanted to collapse in that bed. While she was changing them, the police arrived. The same officers who appeared at her house that morning returned.

They all convened at the dining table. "Enemies, you were telling us earlier that you had enemies. Why don't you tell us about them?"

"Let me help you out," John said. "Security at the Night Hawk put together a list of all the employees who have been fired and the customers who have been kicked out of the casino since Caroline has taken over as general manager." He retrieved a few folded sheets of paper from his pocket.

Dan, the shorter of the two officers, perused the list. "There are over fifty names here. It will take a long time to investigate this many suspects."

"When you run a casino, you make some enemies, in fact, it's a good day if you don't make an enemy," Caroline said. "But a few stand out—the ones who have actually threatened me. I would put Derrick Thomas at the top of the list. There was just something in the way he called me a bitch which gave me chills. Usually when there is an incident, you never see the person again, but he came back to threaten me. He thinks I ruined his life. I have a feeling his hands painted the billboard. Show me the list." She pointed to his name.

The shorter officer checked his notes. "The billboard on the highway that read, 'Caroline Popov must die' sprawled across the front in red paint?"

"Precisely. Finding out who painted that billboard would be the first place to start, guys. Let's leave the lady alone tonight. I think she could use some sleep. I promise we'll come down to the station in the morning." In a firm but polite way, John shut the conversation down and let the officers know they were done asking questions for the evening.

Caroline and John escorted the officers out. A million stars blazed across the sky. Usually the sight of the stars filled Caroline with wonder, but tonight they made her feel small and insignificant. The chill in the air made her shiver and she wrapped her arms around herself.

****

The next morning she woke to a knock on her bedroom door. "Come in," she called. The events of yesterday flashed through her head.

John held a cup of hot chocolate and set it on her bedside table. She picked the cup up and sipped. "This smells delicious and tastes great." She threw on her robe and followed him into the kitchen. "I guess we need to go to the police station, but first I have to visit Erica. She has to know how sorry I am."

"I have glad tidings for you this morning, you aren't going to believe me. The police interrogated Derrick last night, and after a little persuasion he copped to painting the billboard."

"Did he shoot Erica?"

"Not sure. He denies it but doesn't have an alibi for the time Erica was shot. Later, he was at the table at Indio Springs. My buddies over there called me. While he was gambling, Brandon broke into his car and searched for evidence. Don't look at me like I did something illegal, the Indio is also a sovereign nation. We found a burner phone with the texts he had been sending you—*From your biggest fan*—and also a can of red paint. It matched the billboard, all the evidence we needed to know that he painted it. Now he is sitting in jail. I'll make sure he is out of the way while we figure this out."

"But what do you think? I trust your instincts."

"I don't know, but it seems a big leap to jump from vandalism and harassment to attempted murder, but we can't count him out. The police have another theory.

Since Erica was shot right outside the gun range, they checked the place out and discovered some guys at the range had been shooting in an off-limits area. One of them pointed his gun in the air and shot. The police believe a stray bullet from the range hit Erica. They are taking the bullet to forensics in Palm Springs. It might take a few weeks to get the results. In the meantime, they have taken the suspects down to the station for questioning."

She shook her head. "I'm not buying it. What are the odds an errant bullet coming off the gun range would hit the neck of a passenger in the front seat of a moving car? Do you really think it could be true? Seems unbelievable to me. I have to admit, I would breathe a sigh of relief if her shooting wasn't my fault, and if someone wasn't trying to kill me."

"Then breathe a sigh of relief. The odds against a hunter hitting a running deer have to be high, but deer get shot every day. As a precaution until things check out, I'm still going to have Brandon protect you."

****

Over the next week Caroline grew accustomed to having Brandon follow her everywhere she went. Having him beside her made her realize how much she enjoyed the companionship. He even stood outside the bathroom. The only time she was alone was when he outran her on their morning run.

John insisted she take the week off work. Every morning, she visited Erica in the hospital, making sure Brandon tagged along. At first, he tried to stand in the hall like a bodyguard, but Caroline persuaded him to join them. "Nothing will speed Erica's recovery more than a handsome ex-Marine in her room."

The next day they walked in to find an elated Erica propped up on her bed, wearing makeup, looking glamorous, and thrilled to have so closely averted death.

Playing to the male presence, Erica appeared almost giddy. "Caroline, this accident makes me feel so alive. The food here sucks. I'm craving a burger, from our favorite place, and while you're out, can you get me a copy of *Enjoy the Present Now?* I want to feel inspired."

"Well, you're still newsworthy." Caroline held up the Orange County Reporter. She read the headline to Erica. *"Former Reality Show Contestant Shot While Visiting Joshua Tree.* You made the front page of the paper! You are famous." Caroline hoped the attention would please her.

"Almost famous. Reality stars are almost famous," Erica coyly giggled.

Caroline and her constant companion Brandon drove to Cabazon and bought Erica ten burgers from California's famous burger drive-in, where the meat was always fresh never frozen. Then they spent three hours getting her a copy of *Enjoy the Present Now* because the nearest bookstore was in Palm Desert. As the days passed and Erica's health improved, her list of demands grew.

Pulling out of the driveway one morning, Brandon stared straight ahead while he asked, "Do you mind if I buy flowers for Miss Erica?"

Noting his cocoa cheeks covered in a brilliant deep shade of scarlet, Caroline teased, "Brandon, you have a crush."

Secretly she was delighted because Erica would

thrive on the attention. Brandon was perfect, a rugged man, handsome, and always polite, the perfect gentleman. Also, Caroline had been run ragged. She would be thrilled for Brandon to share the burden of taking care of Erica. From that day on Brandon doted on Erica, happy to grant her every wish.

****

Later in the week Erica was released from the hospital. She stayed at Caroline's to rest and regain her strength until she was declared well enough to return home to Orange County.

On their last night together Caroline planned an authentic High Desert experience. At precisely six p.m. Brandon pulled up to the cabin in a van with the Night Hawk logo prominently displayed on the side.

Driving up a twisty mountain road, accompanied by their bodyguard, they arrived at Pioneertown. The one street fit organically into the countryside, surrounded by rust colored rock formations. The town wasn't a ticky-tacky tourist trap, just a deserted movie set built in the heyday of the Western movies, the 1940s, now being lovingly cared for by modern day pioneers. Their residences were caravans and cabins dotted around the hillside.

Once they parked, Brandon opened up the back of the van pulling out a wheelchair. Erica scoffed, "I am perfectly capable of walking."

Even though she protested, Brandon insisted. "I'm not taking any chances, you're riding while you're under my charge."

They took their time strolling down the dusty street past the brothel, next to the saloon, across from the jail, before entering the grounds of Jean & Jessie's. Brandon held the heavy doors open for them as they entered the outside courtyard dotted with wooden tables. The smell of charring meat sizzling on large outdoor pits blasted them as they took their seats. A cowboy playing an acoustic guitar stood on stage serenading the patrons.

She squeezed Erica's hand. "I am so glad we reconnected. I just wish things had turned out better. I hope you'll come again. Maybe you won't get shot next time. Promise we will never lose touch again." The weeks had passed in a blur, by the end their bond had been rekindled.

"I promise, I will. To old friends and new beginnings." Erica spoke to Caroline but her eyes never left Brandon's face. "No drinking, doctor's orders." The girls clinked their glasses together, holding their sparkling waters in the air.

Caroline felt like a third wheel, who Erica and Brandon secretly hoped to get rid of. She planned to disappear soon, leaving a two-wheeler, the happy couple.

After platters of ribs had been devoured, John sauntered up to their table dressed in a skinny suit. "Caroline, I'm so glad you told me you were coming here. I am on my way to the casino. Some red card holders are driving up from Palm Springs, and I want you to schmooze them." He turned to Erica and Brandon. "Do you mind if I steal her?"

She practically skipped all the way to John's car. "As always, you played your part perfectly. I don't know when I've seen you so dressed up. The silk shirt and the tie are almost too much. You even convinced me. I think those two are really into each other. I'm keeping my fingers crossed, I hope something positive comes out of this."

Later that night a sleepy Caroline woke up when Brandon's car turned into her gravel driveway dropping Erica off. Caroline glanced at her bedside clock, the bright red numbers read two a.m. Mission accomplished, she fell back into a contented sleep.

Chapter Twenty-Six

Your Typical Casino Heist Movie Is Logistically Impossible

Movie makers love to portray casino heists as elaborate robberies involving high tech equipment and teams of robbers pulling off complex plots that defy logic. In reality, if one wants to steal from a casino, the best approach is to steal small amounts of money over a long period of time, preferably without cameras watching. Money flows through a casino like the tide. The winnings rise and fall, and until it is counted at the end of the day, nobody really knows how many bills are deposited in the slot machines or the table games' drop boxes.

On Caroline's first day back at the office, she called Mindy to ask for advice. "I can't quite put my finger on the reason, but money seems to be missing. The hold seemed particularly low for the week I was gone."

"Patterns, search for patterns," her friend advised. "Where, what, and most importantly who. Which department do you suspect the theft arises out of, how much has been stolen, and who has access to that money?"

"I think I've already figured some of it out. Someone has been stealing cash from the drop boxes. I don't know how they are getting into them. When the carts carrying the drop boxes travel from the tables or the slot machines to the count room, cameras track them every step of the way. Two keys are needed to open any of the boxes, and one key stays in the count room. Security guards are with the money every step of the way."

"Then security would be the best place to start your search. In Atlantic City they caught a long-time employee stealing when the bank called to alert them that a security guard had deposited over one hundred thousand dollars in cash at the bank over a span of just a few months. To steal, employees have to form alliances. Make sure to cross departments when you investigate. Don't forget to take an audit of all of the departments."

In her mind she tallied up a list of suspects. "I think my search is leading me back to the beginning. Sometimes something which seems really simple, really is."

"Employees across the country are very inventive in thinking up new ways to steal from casinos. Greed is universal because people think they are entitled. Sometimes they think they are overworked and underpaid, but most of the time they are just broke. Once you put your hand in the till, it's hard to stop putting your hand in the till."

"I can't share my suspicions with John until they are confirmed, but I will tell you what I think is going on." She related the details of her investigation to Mindy. After Caroline hung up her phone, she called surveillance and asked to view yesterday's tapes of the games she suspected were being compromised.

Most casinos keep track of the big bills, the fifties and hundreds, but count the smaller bills as part of the "grind." Before any cash is dropped at a table game, the money has to be proven to the camera. By rewinding yesterday's tape, Caroline could track all the money going into the boxes. Carefully watching the screen, she counted every bill dropped into the box on the low limit game, the table with the most grind.

From the time after the drop—big bills and smaller bills—twenties, tens, fives, and even the ones. She calculated the amount of $47,985 had been dropped into the drop box on the low limit game. Comparing that figure against the revenue report on her desk, only $44,234 had been reported as revenue on that game. She picked up her calculator and did the math. It showed three thousand seven hundred fifty-one dollars missing from the drop box.

Where the money went and who had taken it was becoming clear. The thief played a very clever game, stealing just enough not to arouse suspicion.

Chapter Twenty-Seven

The Faster the Dealer the More Revenue for the Casino

Finally, after months of training, the day of the half-marathon arrived. Walking out the door for her last practice run, a quick one, she glanced at her cell phone lying on the bedside table, noticed the power was low, and plugged it into the charger. She picked up the pepper spray and slipped it into her pocket. Caroline breathed in the crisp morning air which signaled winter was fast approaching. She hid a key under the rocking road runner in the front yard. Its body bobbed and shifted as the wind blew up from the valley.

Erica was settled back in Orange County. The two spoke every day and Erica planned to drive up this afternoon to visit Brandon. The investigation into the losses from the drop boxes was firming up. Caroline was confident she'd soon be able to present her evidence to John.

Running down the hill she passed the house where a local artist, Bob, lived in a small stucco octagon hut. His giant bronze horse greeted her. He twisted metal into interesting shapes—windmills, fountains, and abstract works scattered across his front yard. She loved passing by his new creations, a first step in forging bonds with her neighbors. Last week on her way up the hill from her practice run, she bought the aluminum road runner from him.

Surprised, she spotted Hector standing at the side of the road beside the love of his life—the electric car. "Caroline," he yelled. "You have to come with me. There's an emergency at work. We couldn't get you on your phone. Brandon sent me to pick you up. They needed him back at the casino. He'll meet you there."

"I'm sorry. I left my phone at home. It didn't have any power. We usually don't have emergencies this early in the morning. What's going on?"

"A young Marine hit a huge jackpot. He won a hundred thousand K, so you gottta come in and verify the win. I'll give you a ride."

A bullshit detector went off in her head. No way would she get into a car with that man. "No, thanks all the same, I'll go home and get cleaned up, I'll be in soon."

"I insist."

As he spoke, someone snuck up behind her, so quietly she never noticed a large object strike her head before her world went black. She woke up, lying across the back seat of a car. A burlap bag had been placed over her head, and her hands were secured by ropes. It felt like a lead weight was pressing on her skull. The pepper spray was gone.

Rock music playing on the radio station cut to commercial. Suddenly, the familiar, cheery jingle for the local station broadcasting from Twentynine Palms filled the car, which let her know she hadn't been out for long. She was still in the local area. Trying to pick up information from her senses she noticed that the car was traveling down a straight road. After a while the car turned right and stopped in a gravel driveway; she heard stones crunching beneath the tires. She played dead, which wasn't much of a stretch, as they lifted her up and deposited her on a hard concrete floor.

Two hands yanked the bag abruptly from her head. Her eyes darted around the room. They had carried her into a one room shack. The windows were boarded up, but light shone through huge cracks in the weathered wooden walls.

Joanna sat at a worn metal picnic table, the kind you usually find outside. "Hector, you go outside and stand guard. I want to have a chat with our guest."

Once he left, she greeted Caroline with a wicked smile. "Having a pleasant morning?"

How ironic, this was the first time she had ever seen Joanna smile. "My head hurts a bit. I am such an idiot. I figured Hector wasn't capable of planning this on his own, but I never suspected you. You're tribal, you get money every month."

"Not enough. Now it's my turn to ask you some questions. Why couldn't you leave things alone? We could have all gotten along."

"It's your people I am trying to protect. Let me ask you, how could you steal from your own tribe?" Caroline touched her necklace surprised that she wasn't panicked, it was as if the severity of the situation shocked her into a strange state of calm. This couldn't be real, this had to be the middle of a nightmare.

"My tribe, what a joke. You mean those people who never set foot on the Shotowa reservation until there was money to be made. Now, all of a sudden, they want to reclaim their heritage. This you'll understand, I should have been tribal chairman, not John. I am superior in every way, but he has the right DNA, *male*. But now I need to know, who have you told?"

"Everybody," she lied. "I've told everyone who'd listen. You can get rid of me, but it's too late. You won't be able to steal from the casino anymore. But just for curiosity's sake, how did you pull it off?"

"I'll tell you if you tell me how you figured it out."

"Sure, a secret for a secret. I suspected the drop was off, but not by much. Let me guess, your department told you I checked the tapes, that's how you guessed I knew. But how did you get in the boxes to steal?" That information would fit in the last piece of the puzzle.

"I would review the tapes every day to figure what the drop was on the low limit games and then we would exchange that box for a box filled with less money— not a lot less, just enough. We all know it is impossible to get an accurate count on those games because of the grind. You see there are always a few extra boxes on the cart in case some boxes break. The thing is no one checks the cart before it goes out on the floor or after it leaves the count room. As long as all the boxes in the casino were accounted for, everyone stayed happy. Until you showed up."

"Genius," she said, for it truly was. "How did you get access to the second key?"

"You know. When you put the new keys in the count room, you almost put us out of business, but then we came up with the cake caper. When you caught them in the count room, Brandon had already made an impression of the new key in some clay and hid it up his sleeve. I made sure to erase that part of the count room surveillance tape."

Caroline's head began pounding. "Brandon is involved with this? Erica is in love with him."

"If you haven't noticed Brandon is black. Do you really think he would fall for that skinny ass bitch, when he can have a real woman like me with some meat on her bones? Who do you think made him go after that fame whore? He loves me, but we can't tell anyone, conflict of interest. I needed to keep an eye on you, and she was the easiest way. You even let us put cameras on your house, so we kept tabs on you. Erica was our woman on the inside only she didn't know it."

"Okay you got a few thousand a day, but was that enough to risk going to jail?"

"Oh, but you underestimate us. We used all of the money to finance a meth lab. Remember the player you kicked out for racism, you nicknamed him Meth-head? Very perceptive." Caroline nodded. Joanna continued, "In your security report you wrote, *he looked like someone running a meth lab in the desert*. Then I concluded you were an excellent judge of character and not as naïve as you appeared because running a meth lab is exactly what he does."

Caroline studied Joanna's face. She appeared to be getting so much pleasure bragging about stealing from her own tribe. "Why are you telling me all of this? I don't know about those crimes." She couldn't believe that the people John counted on and trusted were all in this conspiracy. Get rid of her and they might get away with the perfect crime. It takes a village to rob a casino, and Joanna thought she had covered all the bases. Her seat in surveillance allowed her to watch security commit their crimes. Her job had been to cover for them.

"I just felt like sharing. No one appreciates my mind, but I reckoned you would. Most of the casino managers before you were alcoholic, womanizing gamblers, happy to have a job. But you were the scariest thing of all, competent." She laughed. "Anyway, you won't be around for long."

"If you're going to kill me, better do it soon. In all the thrillers I've read, if the villains wait too long then the heroine, which will be me, gets rescued." She couldn't believe she was giving advice to her potential killer, but she needed to keep Joanna talking.

"I wish I could get rid of you now, but I have also read enough thrillers to know the corpse always gets found, especially here in the desert. A Marine shot his mistress, and years later they found her. He dumped her in an abandoned well. Bodies don't disintegrate well in the dry heat. The bones last forever. No, I have other plans for you, something crueler, something that will make you wish you were dead. Here, take a bite of this. You will need to keep your strength up." She held a sandwich up to Caroline's face.

"What if it's poisoned?" Caroline was terrified, but she needed to keep Joanna talking.

"It's not." Joanna took a bite out of the sandwich.

Act composed, Caroline told herself. Biting into the turkey sandwich coated heavily with mayo, she studied Joanna's face, staring at all the lines etched into it. They seemed even deeper today, more like tire tracks than a rake.

"I told you I don't want you dead. We already tried to kill you at the gun range. The police will believe that a shooting is accidental once but twice screams attempted murder. Our guy was inside the range shooting in the air, while Brandon was on the road aiming at what we thought was you, only Erica got in the way." Joanna held a bottle of ginger ale with a straw up to Caroline's face.

Caroline gasped like the breath had been knocked out of her, forcing some of the spicy ginger ale to dribble down her chin. Brandon had tried to kill her—the man she trusted, John trusted. She had been so certain of Derrick's guilt that she had to ask the obvious question. "I just have to know, was Derrick working with you guys?"

"No. Meet your biggest fan, it's me, you dummy! We were thrilled when he started stalking you before we even thought about taking you out. Derrick made the perfect patsy. For months we used him and abused him, and he never figured out we were following his every move. He still doesn't know we sent him to your place on the Fourth of July, and now he never will."

"Oh, how did you send in the fake taxi order and then erase it from his phone?"

"Brandon is accomplished at his job, security. He can hack a cell phone in under a minute. Then we planted a burner phone with the texts to you in his car at Indio Springs while he was gambling."

"Clever. Sounds like Brandon is just a jack of all trades." Caroline wondered how many more secrets Joanna would reveal.

"It's a shame you can't share this with John, but unfortunately you are emigrating to Mexico. They don't check trucks going south. Meth-head was delighted to arrange for a member of a Mexican drug cartel to pick you up this afternoon. My plan is brilliant. We are selling you into white slavery. The cartel might be disappointed because let's face facts, you are a little long in the tooth, but they will be happy you are blonde."

She picked up a piece of Caroline's hair in her hand. "This is natural, isn't it? The plan is for them to make some money on you before they dispose of you, by selling you or passing you around to their members, an employee benefit. They probably haven't ever ridden anything as tall as you. Picturing you under some short Mexican drug dealer makes me laugh."

A phone rang. Joanna hastily gagged her before answering. While she talked, Caroline listened for clues. "Yes, I'm really looking forward to the race," she paused. "At home, just drinking coffee on the porch. Have to conserve my energy." After a few minutes more of small talk, Joanna ended the phone call, then ripped the tape off Caroline's mouth.

Again, she held the bottle up to Caroline's lips, keeping her eyes on Caroline the whole time. "I wish I could stay longer, but there is a race this evening and I have to get ready. Remember we all took the day off for the race, so you won't be missed until later. You see how well I planned this? Didn't you wonder why I asked you to race with us? Don't worry, I won't leave you alone. Hector will be here to watch over you. If you hope John is going to save you, I just talked to him, and I don't think he can save you from Palm Springs. Even if he found out where you were, by the time he got up here you'd be on your way to Mexico."

"You won't get away with this," Caroline pleaded as Joanna replaced the bag over her head.

"Maybe not, but with you out of the way, it's just my word against yours. I don't have to tell a smart girl like you that blood is thicker than water, especially Native blood. I'll just convince John you were the one stealing. Hopefully he'll think Derrick kidnapped you, he was released from jail last night, insufficient evidence for attempted murder." Joanna got the last word in before sliding the bag over Caroline's head.

Caroline began to feel drowsy. Suddenly she realized her drink had been drugged, but it was too late. Sometime later, she woke up as her body was hoisted into the air, the burlap bag again covering her head. Then she was thrown into a truck filled with the overpowering stench of rotting fruit and pushed to the back.

Silently she prayed to the universe, 'Someone, please save me. If this truck leaves this driveway, I am well and truly screwed.'

Chapter Twenty-Eight

Diplomacy Gets Ninety Percent of the Job Done

John, a man of many bad habits, held his early morning gin and tonic in his hand as he made his rounds, stopping by each blackjack table asking after his employees' families. He passed by Dave. "How's your wife? Has she dropped her baby yet?" He greeted the customers. "Rachel, what a big stack of chips you've won. How do we stay in business?" He made sure to give his card to the new customers, especially the attractive women.

He was the only tribal chairman who made these daily rounds, but he supposed it made a difference because Shotowa casinos were always voted the number one casino by the Desert Palm readers. Dealing with tribal councils for decades taught him diplomacy got ninety percent of the job done.

Schmoozing was also the perfect excuse to have a drink in the morning.

Noticing a pretty redhead playing a slot machine, he handed her his card. "Hi, I'm John Tovar, tribal chairman here. Call me if you need anything or even if you don't. Let me buy you a drink."

She laughed at his joke. He moved away quickly so as not to come off like a lech. Experience also taught him that it was always better to let the woman make the first move.

His cell phone lit up. He glanced at the screen. Curious, he picked up the call because when the Bureau of Indian Affairs calls, you answered. "Tovar here."

"John, this is Mindy Oxendine. Is Caroline with you?"

"No, I haven't seen her for a few days, but I will this afternoon. I am going up the hill to watch the half-marathon at Joshua Tree."

"Me, too, I just arrived from Washington. She left me a key, and I have been waiting in her living room for over an hour. There is no sign of her, she doesn't answer her phone, and the convertible is in the driveway. I wouldn't usually worry, but with everything that's happened lately I think we should be concerned. Officially I flew in to cheer Caroline on in the race, but really, I am helping her with an investigation. She hasn't told you yet, but she thinks she knows who is ripping off the casino."

"Thank God you told me. Maybe I can find her, everyone in management has a work supplied cell phone which they always carry. Most of them probably don't realize that I can track the location of all the phones for security reasons. Let's hope we can figure out where she is. Call you back."

He pressed Caroline's phone number from the Rolodex on his cell phone. The location tracker indicated her phone was at her house.

He rang Mindy back. "Check the house, I think her phone is there."

A minute passed before she answered him. "I found it in her bedroom. Her phone is plugged in the charger, on vibrate."

"She doesn't have her phone. Now, I am getting worried. I am on my way now, but it will take me awhile to get there from Palm Springs. Stay where you are and I will update you. Meanwhile I'll call the Night Hawk and find out if she showed up to work. Then I'll call you back."

A few minutes later he left the Palm Oasis, heading to his reserved parking spot proudly labeled Tribal Chairman. There sat his sports car, a ridiculous car bought in the midst of his last divorce. He didn't buy new cars to celebrate marriages, just divorces.

"I called the casino. No one has seen her. Mindy, you have to tell me what you know. I have to know what's going on at the Night Hawk."

"I hate to say this, but she suspects Hector has been stealing from the casino. She believes he has an accomplice, but couldn't figure out how, and more importantly who. I came here to help her fit the last puzzle pieces together before she shared her evidence with you. I think someone has kidnapped Caroline." Mindy's words tumbled out in a hurried jumble. She couldn't impart information fast enough.

He hung up the cell phone and immediately called Joanna. "How's life going? Ready for the big race?" Something told him not to ask about Caroline, not until he had her location pinned down.

"Yes, I'm really looking forward to the race."

The tracker on his cell phone was still working, and once he noticed Joanna's location, he understood everything. "Where are you?"

"At home, just drinking coffee on the porch. Have to conserve my energy."

She was lying. She couldn't be on her porch

because she was right outside of Twentynine Palms on the old road to Vegas, an area known as Wonder Valley, an ironic name for an area filled with desolate shacks. He was not certain he could get through the rest of this conversation without screaming, but a lifetime of hiding his feelings helped him stay calm. He couldn't believe that his beloved cousin would lie to him, much less steal from the casino and kidnap Caroline.

After he clicked off, John called his friend at Desert Regional SWAT, an Afghanistan veteran with Special Forces training. John kept the number of all the SWAT teams in the valley on speed dial. When you ran a casino, anything could happen. In 1980 a disgruntled gambler blew up a South Shore casino in Lake Tahoe because the owners didn't pay his ransom demands, and the Las Vegas shootings were always in the back of his mind.

While he redialed Mindy, he thanked God for hands free phones. "I'm coming as fast as I can. Joanna made her first mistake, she forgot I could track her phone. If the satellite is correct, she is in the homestead cabin her father built."

"Homestead cabins. Didn't that end about a hundred years ago?"

"From the depression until 1976 the government would give you five acres if you built a cabin on land in the High Desert. Her father drove here from Chicago, lured by the mystique of the desert. In reality he faced desert scrub, no utilities, and no jobs. Giving up, he moved to Twentynine Palms, found a job and a wife. When we were children, we used to play on the homestead. I learned to shoot rifles and track game from there. You can see hundreds of those shacks on the back road to Vegas. The SWAT team is meeting me out there. Lock the doors. Don't let anyone know you are there. Hold tight where you are."

Making his way along Indian Canyon he passed over Interstate 10. He winced every time he drove by the sign for the *Christopher Columbus Highway,* an affront to all Native people of the Americas. You didn't discover us. We inhabited the land all across this highway, from coast to coast. We didn't need you to find us, we were doing fine without you. The road was famous for carrying the majority of goods across the country in massive trucks rumbling along the highway. He passed over the bridge separating the low desert from the high desert.

He grew up in Palm Springs, the jewel of the Low Desert, playground of the stars. Even at an early age he was aware of how being Shotowa made him different. It sucked to be poor, but on the weekends he played with his cousins in the High Desert, a place so remote that most of its residents never even visited Palm Springs. In Wonder Valley he and his cousins were allowed to run free. He prayed his instincts were right.

Outside of Joshua Tree on the road to Vegas, he began to pass a ghost town filled with row after row of derelict deserted one room wooden cabins, bleached gray by the sun. Torn screens decorated the windows, and doors hung off their hinges. He spotted Joanna's cabin but continued down the road, careful to park his car out of sight behind a cabin three shacks down. The desert was singing its song as the wind began to blow harder, carrying sand through the air. He chose this road because it was near the cabin, a vast area of flat lands surrounded by scrubby brush. He lowered himself to the ground, crawling through the brush as the unrelenting sun beat down on him.

He paused at a rock scarred by a scratch from a bullet. His mind wandered to memories of happy days playing cowboys and Indians with his cousins. Being the youngest, he always got stuck impersonating a cowboy. One day the cousins had been tracking a rabbit across the desert when a rattler appeared on the path, fast as lightning. Joanna fired at the snake, missing John's toes by a few inches—and scaring the bejesus out of him. The girls broke out in laughter when they noticed the stain on his jeans from peeing his pants. A few tears ran down his cheek when he realized what he would have to do to his favorite cousin when he found her.

But then he remembered Caroline and grew furious. He convinced her to get into this business, and she had done a damn fine job. She was honest, hardworking, and loyal. Sometimes he felt like she cared for the Night Hawk more than he did. She had gotten into this fix trying to protect him and the tribe. Damn Joanna, he couldn't let her hurt Caroline. He would kill her if she did. He blamed himself for placing Caroline in danger. Why hadn't he heeded her warnings, taken them more seriously, and acted on them sooner? No wonder all of his marriages were doomed to failure. He didn't know how to listen to women.

Utilizing all of the tracking skills Joanna had taught him, he approached the cabin undetected, zigzagging through the desert, hiding behind the brush and crawling on silent knees. Slithering on his belly, he spotted a truck decorated with painted fruit in the gravel driveway. Peeking inside a large crack in the wall of the cabin, he observed Hector and two other men chomp away on sandwiches, a paper bag lying beside them on the floor. Assault rifles leaned against their chairs. A comatose body lay on the floor covered with a burlap bag. Even from this distance he could detect the blonde hairs peeking out. He could see straight through the cabin because the door was open.

Realizing Hector could never have planned this on his own, he concluded that Joanna masterminded the kidnapping, recalling from his childhood how good she was at manipulating everyone around her.

John prayed the SWAT team had located the place and were now ready for action. He pulled out his cell phone and texted the captain a description of the truck. He placed his faith in the SWAT team because he observed them training many times. Even though Caroline was being guarded by a buffoon, he couldn't charge in on his white horse because he didn't have a horse, and more importantly he didn't have a gun. Unable to do anything, he hid in silence while they finished their sandwiches and lifted Caroline's unresponsive body.

The two men picked her up and carried her out of the shack, holding her as if she was a roll of carpet. They threw her into the back of the truck and slammed the door shut. Hector returned to the cabin. Watching as the truck pulled out of the driveway, John's heart fell to the ground. For the first time in a long time he prayed to the ancient Shotowa Gods.

A few seconds later, sirens accompanied by the sound of gunfire rang out across the desert. At the sound of the guns Hector ran out of the cabin.

Immediately, five officers emerged from the brush surrounding him. John never noticed the officers hiding, pretty impressive tracking.

He ran around to the front of the cabin in time to watch the Twentynine Palms police chief place handcuffs on Hector while the chief recited, "You are under arrest. You have the right to remain silent and to refuse to answer questions. Anything you say may be used against you in a court of law."

John strode up to Hector and read the fear in his eyes. "I'm going to advise you to sing like a bird. Do you really want to go to jail for the rest of your life because Joanna hatched some crazy plan? Knowing my cousin, I'm sure she got the sundae and barely threw you some peanuts. Add the charge of kidnapping to embezzlement, and you are going away for a very long time."

Then John ran up the road to where twenty members of the SWAT team surrounded the produce truck. The officers were removing crates of produce, and then a figure emerged: a relieved, groggy, and shell-shocked Caroline.

"Oh my God! John, you did come. They were planning to take me to Mexico where I would have just disappeared." Arms shaking and talking so fast, he barely understood every other word, she said, "We have to arrest Joanna. There's so much more you don't know the race is in about two hours, we need to be there. You saved my life. Will someone untie me?"

The officer beside her opened the blade of his knife and cut the ropes binding her wrists. She leaned against the police cruiser.

"Ready to take down some more bad guys?" the

chief asked.

The SWAT team cheered. Most of the ex-Marines didn't get much action in the desert, and they didn't want to get rusty.

"Are you sure you want to come with us, Caroline? You've had a rough day. I can't imagine what you have just been through."

"John, I'm fine. No, that's not true. My head is throbbing and my body aches, but I know I won't relax until they are arrested. Brandon is a part of all of this, and Erica is driving up today to watch him run the race. We have to keep her away from him! I can't relax until I know she is safe! Strangely, avoiding being sold into white slavery is slightly exhilarating. I need to see them go down, and besides I'm already dressed for the race, still wearing my running clothes." She sniffed at her clothes and wrinkled her nose. "They stink of rotten fruit."

John interjected, "I just realized the people I care for the most have been screwing me over." He suppressed the tears forming in the corner of his eyes, he didn't have time for self-pity. "We have to make one stop. We have to pick up Mindy. She called me worried when you didn't meet her at your cabin."

"You heard the Shotowa chief. I've always wanted to say this like a Marine—Rah! On to Joshua Tree!" The head of the SWAT team opened the door for John and Caroline. They slid into the back seat of the SWAT team's cruiser.

With a clear sky overhead, the temperature was dropping as sunset approached. At the start of the half-marathon course, hundreds of runners stood milling around the campground where they picked up their bibs and race packets. In less than thirty minutes the race would begin. To light the path, the runners wore head lamps. The sun would set at five-forty-nine p.m., and the race would start at six-fifteen. John approached the crowd on his own, searching for Joanna. He spotted her and Brandon placing their running bibs printed with their entry numbers around their necks. For the first time John noticed the vibrations between the two of them. Caroline is right. Why didn't I see it? They are together. "Hey, Cuz, good luck in the race, and you too, Brandon. Seen anyone else here?" He baited her. "I know Caroline signed up to run."

"I haven't seen her. Maybe she got tied up at work." Joanna and Brandon shared a smile at what they believed was their private joke, but John planned on having the last laugh.

Caroline slipped in beside them, her entry bib hanging around her neck. The surprised expression on Joanna's and Brandon's faces told John everything he needed to know.

"Get them, guys!" He held his hand up in the air. At the signal, the SWAT team all wearing bibs morphed out of the crowd, surrounded the kidnappers, and handcuffed them.

Enraged, Caroline walked over to Joanna and Brandon standing shackled for all the runners to see. "I always worried because of my job someday someone would come to hurt me, but I never dreamed it would be the two of you."

Precisely then, Erica came from up the road joining them, "Sorry I'm late. There was so much traffic on the Sixty. Why is Brandon in handcuffs?"

"I have so much to tell you. Sorry, Brandon is not

who we thought he was. But I'll fill you in when we get back to the cabin."

As the sun set behind the mountains, a gunshot boomed through the desert signaling the start of the race. The marathoners began their way meandering through a hard thirteen miles of packed dirt circling the national park. Caroline confessed to John and Mindy, "Next year, I promise you I will run, next year."

"So you're going to continue to work for me? You aren't going to quit? This hasn't scared you off?"

"Naw, I don't want to miss out on any of the action. I'm getting used to being an honorary Shotowa, besides you need me."

As the runners ran through the desert, blazing stars leading their way, Caroline, Mindy, Erica, and John climbed into the back of police cruisers and took a trip to the Twentynine Palms police station, sirens blasting for the entire ride.

Chapter Twenty-Nine

British Dealers Are the Gold Standard, Sometimes What You Find is Fool's Gold

The first hour of the drive back from Vegas on the back roads of the Mojave Desert you pass the old Post Office in the ghost town of Cima. Farther down the road you turn at the Kelso train depot to arrive at the iconic Route 66 sign in front of the gas station in Amboy. Derrick had grown up California dreaming in London, but those dreams included sandy beaches and hot girls in bikinis, not three hours of a deserted road no cars in sight. The kind of road that can make a man, more self-aware than he, think about why his life veered from the straight and narrow path.

Passing by all the abandoned shacks in Wonder Valley gave him the willies. The high moon illuminated rows of abandoned cabins, giving the area a ghostly quality. He contemplated the individual stories of hope that led people there and the frustration that made them leave. Knackered, searching for company, he tuned in the local classic rock station. In a nostalgic mood, he hoped to hear a fave from his glorious youth.

His trip to Vegas had been a bust. He didn't know how the word spread, but even though his CV was impressive, there were no takers. Not even a bite as a floorman. To his surprise, a few days ago, the sheriff released him from jail, no explanation other than the charges had been dropped. It had also been not so politely suggested that he leave the area to avoid further trouble with the law. Trying to oblige, he made the trip to Sin City, searching for employment. While there he managed to turn his last thousand into a hundred dollars. He couldn't afford to lose all his money, he needed to fill his car tank up with gas for the ride back.

After a Led Zeppelin classic about a stairway in the sky finished, the announcer broke in, "*My night owls, this is Magnificent Mike. I know you are out there. Call and let me know what you think of the developments over at the Night Hawk that have rocked the valley.*"

The sound effect of shattered glass filled the air before Magnificent Mike continued. "*Who would have believed that the head of security, Brandon Boyd, would conspire with the Chairman's cousin to kidnap the Casino Manager Caroline Popov? I know my listeners play there, what else is there to do in this valley? Let me know if you have had contact with any of the accused. Just remember, night owls, the man is innocent until proven guilty.*" He repeated the phone number for the radio station.

Derrick's body recoiled. Gobsmacked, he immediately ordered his mobile to call the station. The only employee working at the small local radio station, Magnificent Mike picked up the call himself. "What do you have to add to the story at the Night Hawk?"

Derrick began to rage, "That fucking Brandon, he stitched me up. I was the table games manager and he threatened me with jail when they fired me." He realized how he had been played. "He must have set up that taxi order that sent me to Caroline's house, and then he beat the shit out of me. I can't say I would have shed a tear if she died, that fucking bitch. Of course he's fucking guilty."

"Watch the language," Magnificent Mike warned him. "We don't want to get fined by the FCC. What is your name, first names only? It seems like you have an interesting story to tell. Did you say you were the table games manager? Night Owls, keep listening. I have a good feeling this is going to be a memorable show."

"Pardon my language, let me not be vulgar here, Brandon is a shnakey shitehawk. Your finest Irish insult for an asshole. Just call me Derrick from Donegal." Then he proceeded to delight the listeners with the sorry tale of how he got snookered.

The next day Derrick lounged on the couch, Guinness in one hand, remote in the other. He kept flipping between the Southern California channels. From Los Angeles to San Diego, the Night Hawk and the heroic rescue of Caroline Popov by the handsome tribal chairman was a headline story on all the channels, their faces plastered across the screen. It was even a feature on the cable news network's tickertape.

"Fuck you all!" he screamed at the screen. "You should have all been shipped to Mexico."

Suddenly homesick, what was keeping him in this fucking country? His California dream had morphed into a nightmare. He hadn't seen the oul fella and the oul wan for a donkey's year. Tears forming in his eyes, he dialed his mobile.

When his Ma answered, he burst into tears. "Ma, could you send me some money so I can buy a plane ticket? I'm skint. You won't believe what they tried to do to your boy. I can be a bit of a chancer, but they tried to blame me for attempted murder, I could never kill anyone. They even threw me in the nick! Your boy needs to see your fair face. I want to come home."

His ma was blubbering on the other line. "Of course, Son, come home. You just need your ma to make you a cuppa and listen to all your troubles. Tell me what you need. I'll find the money."

"I'll be glad to leave this fecking country." He would never curse to his ma. She would show him the back of her hand if he did.

"It's not what it is cracked up to be, Ma. Nothing is made here. All the shite you buy is from China. Public transportation is nonexistent. They don't even have a National Health System. If you get sick and don't have money, they'll just let you die. Mass shootings every day. Sometimes you're scared to go outside." He threw in the last bit to up the drama level.

It took Derrick a few days to sell his car and the few possessions that weren't destined for the refuse bin. By the morning of his flight, he had condensed his worldly goods into two suitcases. What kind of stupid bloke leaves America worse off than when he arrived?

The streets weren't paved in gold, they were lined with shite. His plan was to go back to London and work at a casino, if he still had his gaming license. A job would keep him on the straight and narrow. If you work in a casino in Britain, you aren't allowed to gamble at any of them.

The joke was on him. All those years ago he made his grand exit, vowing never to return. Now he couldn't wait to get back to the land of the Sassenach, into the loving arms of his ma, the only woman in the world who wasn't a bitch. He was older, but he was none the wiser. Eager to fly away into the sunset, when the taxi dropped him off at the Palm Springs airport, he didn't even turn around.

Chapter Thirty

Sometimes You Win, Sometimes You Lose, and Sometimes You Hit the Jackpot

A few weeks passed before life at the Night Hawk began to calm down. Everyone had been shocked when the conspiracy was exposed to reveal an epic story containing all the elements of great tabloid fodder— tribal members stealing from their tribe, meth manufactured in the desert like an episode of *Cooking with Meth.* Throw in kidnapping and white slavery, and it was the story that kept on giving.

Employees found themselves repulsed and excited to find their casino the focus of a national scandal, but some of the enthusiasm damped down because Night Hawk policy prohibited employees from talking to the press. Brandon broke Erica's heart, but being featured on the front-page cover of *Almost Famous People* magazine helped assuage the grief a little. Since she was not an employee of the casino, Erica happily talked to anyone and everyone.

Eventually, the television cameras left town, and Caroline returned to work. The casino floor packed, a disc jockey spinning tunes, smoke wafting through the air, just another Saturday night. Wandering through the casino on the way to her office, an explosion of bells and whistles filled the casino. She flinched a bit, still jumping at the sound of loud noises. Caroline followed the sound. The high-pitched scream of an ecstatic Holly pierced the room.

"I won, I won!" Holly screamed while jumping up and down. "My astrology worked!" The display flashed jackpot pending, the amount just shy of a million dollars. Jumping up and down she kept repeating, "I'm rich! I'm rich!"

"I'm so thrilled for you." Caroline really meant it.

She adored Holly. When a local won a big jackpot the publicity would drive in more business, a win-win for everyone. "You know this is going to take a long time to verify, but you just hang in and we'll get your money to you."

Caroline stayed by her side while surveillance ran through the tape, and security reset the machine. An hour passed before John arrived. The jackpot was so huge that he needed to sign off on it, give the final approval, and supervise the payout, but most importantly to pose with Holly for the photo the casino would hang on the winners' wall.

The last few weeks had been tough on John. As chief of the Shotowa Tribe he made sure that the FBI arrested Joanna, Brandon, and Hector. They were thrown into a federal prison. Since they were being charged with kidnapping, bail had been denied. They were facing life sentences, and the Shotowa nation wouldn't be satisfied with anything less. Before being incarcerated, Joanna pleaded for John to take care of Ahote. Although John was disappointed in his cousin, he loved her son, so he agreed to take custody. Taking care of him cured John's restlessness in a way failed marriages couldn't.

John spoke softly to Caroline, "You need a break. Go to the Chop House, and I'll meet you once the jackpot is paid. Hey, by the way, Ray Gordon wants to make a television movie about you. He says that a movie will really attract customers to the Night Hawk, put it on the map. I have only one condition, he has to title it *Casino Queen.*"

"Okay, but I guess since it's only a television movie, I won't be famous just almost famous." Not really believing anything would come of it.

John chuckled. "By the way, there is an old customer in the restaurant who wants to speak with you. A long time ago he asked me to take care of you, and with a few exceptions I think I've done a pretty good job."

Freshening up for dinner, she stopped by her office to reapply her lipstick and straighten her scarf. Walking in the restaurant, her heart stopped, she spied Andrei sitting at a booth in the back corner.

She had dreamed of this moment every day since she abandoned him, but suddenly facing him in the flesh panicked her. Terrified, she almost turned around and walked out. Even from a distance she could tell that he had lost some of his cockiness, and there were crinkly lines around his eyes, but he still made her heart race.

Deciding to face her future, she ran to the booth scared to blink, scared he would disappear. "Can you forgive me?"

"Can you forgive me?" Tears began to form in both of their eyes. "Your nametag says Caroline Popov. You are still a Popov."

"Always only you." She slid into the booth beside

him. "How did you know where to find me?"

"John. After you left Russia, I looked through my wallet and found the business card John gave me. I called him. Knowing that you were working for John I took as a sign you would be okay. John would be watching over you. Every month I call him to make sure you are still okay. I make him promise not to tell you, not to spoil your new life. Then he told me you still loved me. He told me everything." He rested his hand on the table.

She placed her hand on top of his, thrilled that the electricity between them was still there. "Everything. I am so relieved. Now you know I didn't cheat."

"I know. For many years I lost my way, but slowly I was working up my courage to come and get you. My green card expired, so I waited for a visa. But when I found out you were kidnapped, nothing could stop me from coming, now!" He banged his hands on the table. "I don't know how, but John pulled some strings and expedited my visa. I picked it up yesterday, and today I am here. Screw my pride, I will do anything if you give me another chance." He pleaded with his eyes and his words.

Her dreams had come true, Andrei the real person, not the fantasy, sat right in front of her. He still banged on tables, he still loved her. She had gotten her do over, and this time she would do it right. Their reconciliation wouldn't be easy. Life had taught her that she could take care of herself, but she had never wanted anyone so much in her life. Always only him.

"Does this mean I finally get my happy ending?"

He nodded his head yes, tears streaming down both of their faces.

"Why am I crying? I am so happy!" At that moment colors became brighter and lines were sharper because Andrei had returned to Caroline's world.

A word about the author...

Growing up in a straight-laced Southern family, I was always fascinated with casinos. In my twenties on a summer hiatus from teaching in North Carolina, I drove to California and became a dealer at Caesars in Lake Tahoe. Well, I can tell you that after teaching high school, handling an unruly gambler was a piece of cake. My mother highly disapproved of my working in a casino, "a place so bad it has 'sin' in the middle."

Eventually, I succumbed to pressure from the family and returned east to take a high-tech job in Boston. I also began working on my MFA in writing at Emerson. I wanted to write the first realistic novel about casino life from the perspective of an experienced table games dealer.

While in Boston I was offered the opportunity to join Princess Cruises as a croupier. Jumping at the chance, I spent the next five years circling the globe. Sometimes life exceeds your dreams. I was awed by the wonders of Venice, the fjords of Norway, and the Hermitage in St. Petersburg.

I returned from ships with a very special souvenir, my Scottish husband Ray. We went to work at a Native American Casino in Palm Springs. We now live in Hollywood, Florida, where I write about my casino years while gazing wistfully out at the ocean.

www.ingramcontent.com/pod-product-compliance
Lightning Source LLC
Chambersburg PA
CBHW060541260626
47161CB00003B/993